NIGHT TRAIN TO PARIS

NIGHT TRAIN TO PARIS

MANNING COLES

CARROLL & GRAF PUBLISHERS, INC.
New York

First Carroll & Graf edition 1985

Carroll & Graf Publishers, Inc.
260 Fifth Avenue
New York, NY 10001

ISBN: 0-88184-205-2

Manufactured in the United States of America

Contents

1

AT SEA

THE BIG CABIN CRUISER rushed on through the darkness, the faint glimmer from the binnacle lamp showing nothing but the face of the man at the wheel like a mask hung upon a black wall. The sky was overcast though occasionally a rent in the clouds showed for a moment a few stars covered again at once as the hurrying rack streamed across. The sea was getting up; the steady hiss of the bows cutting through the water was more and more frequently interrupted by the heavy spatter of spray upon the deck.

A second man entered the small wheelhouse and bent over the binnacle to see the time by his wrist watch.

"No sign of her yet?" said the helmsman.

"Of course not. Much too early."

"Sea's going up. What was the last weather report?"

"More gale warnings," said the man with the wrist watch. "Going to be a real blow, Alton."

"What did you call me?"

"Sir."

"That's better," said Alton smoothly, and walked away.

"Thinks he's still in the ruddy Navy," said the helmsman to the floating compass which immediately slewed several points to port as a vicious cross sea caught the little ship abeam. "Come up, you cow. Glad it isn't me goin' to be picked off a ship on a night like this."

Nearly an hour later he saw a distant light and opened his mouth to shout, but before he could speak a strong light awoke in the bows of the cabin cruiser as Alton switched on the searchlight and swung it vertically upwards. He shouted down to the second engineer to come on deck and then came himself to take the wheel.

"Go and lend Dick a hand, Johnny. Fender's out on the portside."

The ship came on, showing first the green starboard light and then a row of lighted portholes. She was visibly slowing down; the cabin cruiser turned to meet her and then swung round in a wide circle to starboard. Dick at the searchlight brought it down until the side of the ship was bright in the glare of it; faces looked over the rail and a long rope ladder fell down the ship's side, unrolling as it came. The ship was rolling heavily; the end of the rope ladder was dipped in the sea, snatched out and dipped again and again. The cabin cruiser, slowed down till she had only just steerageway, was being thrown about like a toy. They drew nearer together, a rope was flung from the steamer, missed, and flung again. This time Johnny caught it.

A short stout figure began to climb slowly down the ladder with occasional stops to look down at the sea. The ladder swung out from the ship's side and smacked back again while the man clung frantically and shouted something.

"Come on!" bellowed Alton. "Come on!" He brought the cabin cruiser close alongside and Dick ran to the foot of the ladder, but it was snatched from him by a roll of the ship.

The man on the ladder came down almost to the end and hesitated, as well he might. The roll swung him out towards the waiting boat and Alton yelled to him to let go and jump. He left it just too late, let go as the return roll started and fell headlong into the sea between the ship's side and the hull of the cabin cruiser.

He was dragged out gasping, crowing and spitting sea water; Johnny brought him to the wheelhouse while the line was cast off, the cabin cruiser turned away from the ship and the engine revolutions speeded up. The searchlight clicked out, the ship's lights retired into the darkness of the night and were surprisingly soon lost to view.

The passenger, sea water pouring off him, clung to the side of the wheelhouse and said in English with a strong German accent that he was wet, very wet. And cold. He was also, rather unexpectedly, clutching the sort of brief case which businessmen carry to the office.

"Take the wheel, Johnny," said Alton, and gave him his course. "You come below and have a drink," he added, addressing the passenger, "you'll be all right. Sea water never hurt anybody except by drowning. This way."

The small saloon was warm and stuffy; merely to be out of the tearing wind was a relief, and the lines of strain began to fade out on the passenger's face. Alton poured out a handsome tot of rum, the stranger drank it straight off and managed to smile.

"Now that my teeth stop chattering," he said, "I introduce

myself. Doctor of Physics Ignatius Muntz, formerly of the University of Heidelberg." He bowed.

"My name is Alton and I am in command of this large ship," said Alton, with a friendly smile. "You want to get those wet clothes off. Just a minute."

He called up the companion ladder and the second engineer came running down, a young man in the very early twenties with sandy hair and eyebrows and a freckled face always ready to grin. It was his first trip with Alton and he was very anxious to please; he was an odd contrast to his black-haired skipper whose lean frame and sallow skin with deep creases running from nostrils to mouth made him look older than his twenty-eight years. His eyes were dark, deep-set under heavy brows and a little too near together, and his mouth shut into a thin line with the lower lip slightly protruding. Dr. Muntz looked from one to the other.

"Dick," said Alton, "Dr. Muntz is soaked to the skin and I think you are the only man with a spare suit on board."

"Certainly, I'll get it. And vest and shirt. Anything I can do——" He opened a door at the far end of the saloon and went out.

"Have some rum," said Alton. "Finest thing in the world to stop a chill from developing." He poured out a second tot and Muntz drank a little of it.

"Strong," he said. "Very strong. Ah! Now I remember something, something most important——"

He put his brief case upon the table; it was attached to his left wrist by a short length of cord which he began to untie.

"In case I drop it coming down that ladder," he explained.

"I did wonder how you had managed to keep hold of it," said Alton.

"If I had not, if it had gone away in the sea, I might as well have gone with it."

"So important as that," said Alton.

"So important as that," agreed Muntz, opening the case. There was a little water in it which he tipped out on the floor and then drew out a flat package wrapped in oil silk with rubber bands round it. He slipped them off and opened the package, which contained several sheets of paper closely folded; he unfolded them carefully. There were scale drawings of some long cylindrical object, so much was obvious at a glance ,but there were also immensely detailed drawings of complicated mechanisms and fittings which conveyed nothing whatever to Alton.

The second engineer returned with an armful of clothes.

"Sorry to have been so long, sir. Couldn't find any socks."

Muntz was too busy examining his papers to take any notice. "A little damp here, a corner where the water has entered," he complained.

"They will soon dry down here," said Alton. "Let's get those wet clothes off you. Finish your rum first, you're shivering."

Muntz drank it off and submitted like a child to having his soaked clothes pulled off him, being rubbed down with a rough towel and dressed again in Dick's dry garments. The process was awkward in the extreme as the space in the saloon was very cramped, the cabin cruiser was apparently trying to stand on her head and roll at the same time like a dog which has just been bathed, and Muntz seemed to have lost any sea legs he ever had. Evidently the rum was taking hold upon him, for his face became flushed and he talked without ceasing.

"I am obliged to you so very much for all your kind acts," he said. "I knew if I to England could get I should among good friends be, and it was true, for here I am on an English ship and the so-kind friends are here before me. Also the papers, my impossible-to-be-overestimated papers. I, thank you from the bottom of my heart. Others also. Your Mr. Churchill will thank you. Your Government will thank you. Your people, when they of it come to know, will selephade—salunade——" He abandoned his English and continued in a flood of German which was only terminated when, at the awkward moment of putting him into Dick's trousers, a salmon-like leap of the cabin cruiser hurled all three men into a heap by the door.

The shock seemed to sober Muntz temporarily and he helped to dress himself in a thick jersey and a coat. He sat down at the table, folded up the papers which were not really damp enough to hurt them, and wrapped them again in their oil-silk cover. He slipped on the rubber bands and patted the packet affectionately, while the other two men stood round the table watching him.

"Better lie down for a bit," suggested Alton. "You might be badly hurt falling about."

Muntz looked up and his eyes were glassy.

"This packet," he said thickly, "the Russians would give one million pounds sterling for this packet. One million pounds. Sterling. But they shan't have it." His eyes focussed with difficulty upon the second engineer.

"That's right," said Dick consolingly. "They shan't have it, then. You take it to London and give it to Winston Churchill yourself."

Some other thought took possession of Muntz, an overpowering and unpleasant thought. He yawned suddenly, changed colour, and sweat broke out upon his forehead.

"Hot in here," he said, "very hot." He rose slowly to his feet, holding the edge of the table.

"He's going to be sick," said the second engineer, and dived into the next cabin for a suitable vessel. But Muntz did not wait; he staggered towards the door with the packet still in his hand.

"Fresh air," he said. "Be all right on deck." He opened the door and in doing so dropped the packet, which Alton picked up for him.

"Give it to me," said Muntz.

"I've put it in your pocket," said Alton, pushing his hand well down into the pocket so that Muntz could feel it. "That's quite safe. Up you go; hold on with both hands, I'll help you."

With Alton pushing behind they arrived at the top of the companion ladder and the wild night sprang at them like an animal. Muntz was whirled, staggering, to the lee rail; Alton, at the head of the companion, could just distinguish the bent and shuddering form. Alton laughed shortly and went below again.

"He seemed to prefer being alone," he said, "so I left him."

"May be all right in a few minutes," said Dick, busily collecting sodden garments from the floor. "Takes 'em like that sometimes. He'll get the sea water out of his system anyway."

"Probably that was what did it," said Alton. "I'm just going up to the wheelhouse, I won't be a minute."

"Very good, sir," said Dick professionally. He piled the soaking clothes in a heap and lay down on a bunk to read an Edgar Wallace till it should be time to go on duty.

Alton went out on deck; there were none of the crew about except the man in the wheelhouse for'ard and he had his back turned. His head and shoulders were faintly silhouetted against the binnacle light and he was plainly fighting with the kicking wheel, he would not look round. Muntz was an indistinct heap of misery near the stern, crouched over the rail. Alton took three silent strides towards him, grasped his ankles and with one strong lift heaved him overboard where a rising wave received him before he had time to cry out.

Alton turned almost in the same motion and went forward along the deck, walking heavily; to Dick in the saloon below it seemed as though his captain had but paused at the head of the ladder before going forward. Alton spoke to Johnny at the wheel for a few minutes and then returned to the saloon.

"Passenger all right, sir?" asked Dick, looking up from his book.

"He seemed to be busily occupied," said Alton. "I didn't interrupt."

He lit a cigarette, picked a book out of a rack on the wall and lay down upon the other bunk. Some little time passed before Dick swung his legs to the floor and sat up. Alton looked across at him with raised eyebrows.

"I was wondering, sir, if the old chap was all right. He's been up there some time and it's pretty cold."

"I was beginning to wonder myself," said Alton. "Better bring him down."

The second engineer nodded and went out. Alton waited while the door was shut and steps sounded upon the companion ladder, then he sat up sharply, took Muntz's waterproof packet out of his coat pocket and, pulling up his jersey, stowed it away inside his shirt. Hasty steps sounded overhead; he buttoned up his shirt, pulled down his jersey and was lying at ease once more as the door burst open and Dick rushed in.

"He's not on deck, sir, Johnny hasn't seen him, he's not in the engine room——"

Alton sat up slowly, staring. "Good lord, he must have——"

"Must have gone overboard, sir——"

"I'll come myself."

They searched the cabin cruiser thoroughly but, rather naturally, did not find Muntz anywhere.

"He must have hung too far over the rail and gone in," said Dick. "It's easily done and she has been rolling all ends up."

"I ought to have brought him down myself, when I went up to speak to Johnny," said Alton, sitting down heavily. "I did think of it, but——"

"Bad business, sir," said Dick sympathetically. "Will there be trouble over this?"

"Oh, I expect so," said Alton wearily. "There's one bright spot, we can carry straight on now and come in by daylight; I didn't fancy putting him ashore in the dinghy in this weather. You've lost your clothes, Dick."

"Oh, that," said Dick indifferently.

Eight hours later Stephen Alton landed at Wapping and came up a side street from the stairs he generally used. At the corner where the side street joined the main road he paused, debating whether to travel by tram or walk to the station and go by train.

Twenty yards from Alton's corner a constable upon his beat anda police sergeant upon his rounds were standing together, talking. The sergeant noticed Alton as he paused at the corner and said: "See that man there?"

To reach the station Alton would have to pass them; he decided against it. A tram came clattering along the road; Alton signalled it, swung himself on board as it slowed down, and turned his back to the police as he was borne past them.

"Who is he?" asked the constable.

"Name of Alton, Stephen Alton. You'll know him when you see him again. Notice what he does when you do see him, where he goes and who he's with. We'll get him one of these days."

"What's he been up to?"

"We can't prove it, but the Inspector's pretty sure he's in all or some of these dock robberies we've had lately. Particularly the robberies from lighters; they're done by someone who knows the river well and he does. Someone who even knows which lighter to pick out of a string of 'em."

"There was all those cases of cigarettes went last week," said the constable.

"Ah. And lots of other things too. Been going on a long time, before you came here. He's got away with it so far, but one of these days he'll slip up and we'll get him, my lad, we'll get him. He's got something on his conscience now; he was coming this way and changed his mind when he saw us, you saw that yourself."

"Yes," said the constable.

"Keep on keeping on," said the sergeant.

2

PEPPER AND SPICE

EDWARD JOHN LOGAN, Merchant, had offices in Mincing Lane in the City of London where he dealt in coffee and spices. They were small dark rooms where the electric light burned continuously throughout the working day, and they were not very well ventilated, so that the air was always heavy with a harmony of ginger, nutmeg, cloves, mace, cinnamon and caraway seeds with the smell of coffee as a ground base. Samples of these were kept in a closet called the storeroom; every time the storeroom door was opened a fresh wave of piquancy drifted into Logan's office. His secretary, Nancy Davie, used to say that it was necessary to change down to the skin and have a bath when she reached home at night in order to lose the scent of business and even then it clung to her hair.

Logan was a man in the forties, tall and well set up, dark-haired and with good features, but beginning to show that loss of elasticity which besets men who lead sedentary lives in stuffy offices. His physical reactions were slowing down and his mind was stiffening into grooves. He lived in an expensive flat near Regent's Park with a manservant who was all that bachelors dream of and so seldom find. In a word, Logan was much too comfortable and was beginning to suffer for it.

On a day about two months after the unfortunate Muntz disappeared into the dark North Sea, Logan returned to his office after lunch, put his gloves in his bowler hat, hung it up with his neat umbrella upon their usual peg and rang the bell for his secretary. She came in at once with her hands full of papers.

"Er—Miss Davie—oh, those are my letters, are they? I'll just sign them."

He went through them hastily, signing one after another without reading them, and Miss Davie's eyebrows went up. This was unlike Mr. Logan, but he had been unsettled in manner for several days. There was something in the wind, could he be getting married? Not very likely; this unsettlement was definitely not rapturous. No secret smiles, no song at the lips, no lightness in the tread.

"Mr. Cogsworth rang up; he would like to see you this afternoon if convenient," she said.

Logan looked up at her. No, definitely not happy. His expression was worried, even hunted.

"Oh, I can't see him this afternoon. Ring him up and ask him to come tomorrow, will you?" Logan pushed back his chair, locked the drawers of his desk, put the keys in his pocket and got up. "I have to go out this afternoon," he added, taking down his hat and umbrella. "I shall not be back here today."

"Very good," said Miss Davie dutifully. Then something irresolute in his manner led her beyond the normal limits of office routine and she added impulsively: "I hope there is nothing wrong?"

"What? Oh no, nothing. At least, nothing that a little firmness will not cure," he said with sudden acidity. "Good afternoon, Miss Davie—er—and thank you." He smiled suddenly, put his hat on for the purpose of taking it off to her, hung his umbrella on his arm and walked out into the street.

"Dear me," said Miss Davie thoughtfully.

Edward Logan was going to see his lawyer who inhabited offices so like his own that but for their being on the first floor and not smelling of spices he would hardly have noticed any change in his surroundings.

"Good afternoon, Logan, pleased to see you," said the lawyer, and shook hands warmly.

"Good afternoon, Fenchurch." Logan put down his hat, gloves and umbrella on one chair, sat down slowly on another and looked across the desk at his old friend.

"Well," said Fenchurch, smiling, "what can I do for you?"

"I've been a fool," said Logan abruptly. "What are you laughing at?"

"I thought you were going to say that. There is a faintly sheepish aspect about you this afternoon which is immediately recognizable to any experienced solicitor. It is almost invariably accompanied by the form of words you have just uttered. Or some equivalent synonym."

Logan scowled for a moment and then laughed.

"No doubt you're right. The world is full of people like me. You've got my will, haven't you, Fenchurch?"

"Certainly. You want to look at it? I'll have it brought in." He touched a bell upon his desk, said: "Mr. Logan's will," to the clerk who answered it, and leaned back in his chair.

"I want to tear it up," said Logan energetically. "With my own hands."

"Why not? It's your will," said Fenchurch. "It's also my poor but honest way of making a living." The clerk came back with the will and Fenchurch opened it. "It's very short."

"Give it to me," said Logan, "and may I borrow your wastepaper basket? Thank you. Now," said Logan, tearing the will into small pieces, "I suppose I'd better tell you the rest of the story since I want your advice."

"There are three things," said Fenchurch, taking off his glasses and rubbing them with a corner of his handkerchief, "about which men most commonly make fools of themselves: namely, horses, cards and women. People don't bet on horses as they did, I suppose there isn't the money, and cards have practically gone out compared to the customs of even fifty years ago. But by some dispensation of Providence which I may admire but cannot understand, there seem to be more women about than ever." He put his glasses on and blinked through them at Logan. "Is that your experience also?"

"It isn't the number of women that worries me," said Logan. "It's just one."

"You're lucky," said Fenchurch, "it's generally two. Well now, what about it?"

Logan explained that he had met Elizabeth Alton about three years earlier and was attracted by her calm manner and general air of competence, her clear mind and exact way of speaking. Fenchurch raised his eyebrows but did not interrupt. Logan said that they had seen a good deal of each other and that he had asked her several times, both verbally and in writing, to marry him but she had always put him off. Not a flat refusal, but a postponement; someday, not yet, not just now. They were not even formally engaged. "This has been going on for a long time now," said Logan indignantly, "more than two years, to be exact, and I'm getting very tired of it. Besides, to tell you the truth, I was desperately keen on it at one time but I'm by no means so keen now. It—it takes the edge off one's enthusiasm to be continually held off and disappointed."

Fenchurch nodded. "It does, it does. The lady never tells you what the impediment is, if there is one?"

"No. I asked her bluntly once whether she was married already and she assured me she was not. I believe her, I don't think for a moment that she is. That is, of course, the obvious suggestion, but I don't think it's the right one in this case."

Fenchurch said nothing and Logan went on.

"About nine—no, ten months ago I took her out in my car one Sunday; we went for a run down to Shere in Surrey. Well, as you know, Greene generally drives me—I don't care for driving and I know I'm not good at it—but on this occasion I left him behind and drove the car myself. I was showing off, actually, no doubt," said Logan with an embarrassed laugh. "Well, on the way back there was a misunderstanding at a crossroads and I ran into a lorry. The car was badly damaged but we were not much the worse, physically, that is; it was Betty's nerves which were severely affected."

Fenchurch imagined being driven in Sunday traffic in Surrey by a driver who himself admitted he was not very good. He sympathized with Miss Alton's feelings even before the crash, but did not say so. .

"She was under the doctor's care for weeks and weeks," said Logan. "She had to give up her employment—she was private secretary to a Member of Parliament—so, as it was all my fault that she couldn't earn, I thought it only right to make her an allowance until she was quite well again."

"I see," said Fenchurch.

"I mean, it was just that and nothing more; I mean, it was my fault that she was incapacitated, it was merely a temporary arrangement during her illness——"

"I quite understand," said Fenchurch.

"Well, so far as I can see, she is quite fit again and if I ask what the doctor says she says he is quite pleased with her. But she doesn't seem to be making the least effort to get another post and I'm sure she could, she's so extremely competent and well trained. I have a certain delicacy about the matter, but the fact is, Fenchurch, I'm beginning to wonder how long it's going on."

"I don't wonder. I should do the same in your place."

"Then there's another thing. I said that I'm sure she's not married, but I'm beginning to think there's another man hanging about."

"Ah."

"Once when I went there the room smelt of tobacco smoke. Betty smokes, but only mild cigarettes and not many of them. This was quite different, really strong tobacco. Another time when I called unexpectedly she was darning socks. Thick woollen socks, Fenchurch. When I asked her about them she laughed and said I'd surprised her in one of her little charities. Do women darn socks for charity, Fenchurch?"

"I'll ask my wife, she is much occupied with what are called 'good works.' Knit, yes, I've seen her doing it, but darning I doubt."

"So do I," said Logan energetically. "In fact, I doubt a lot of things these days. One evening when I was there her doorbell rang. There are three floors of flats; each tenant has his own doorbell as usual, and Betty's on the first floor. She went down to answer the door and while I was waiting I strolled to the window, quite idly, as one does, you know. A man went away from the door and as he left he turned on the pavement and waved his hand. Like this. Quite carefree and friendly, damn him. He didn't raise his hat, he waved to her. Then she came upstairs again and said it was a man who'd come to the wrong address. I asked if it were anyone she knew and she said, 'Oh no. A total stranger.' He didn't behave like a total stranger, that's all."

"Perhaps he was merely being impertinent," said Fenchurch.

"It's possible, I suppose," said Logan sulkily.

"Tell me," said Fenchurch. "Since you seem to be thoroughly tired of the whole business, is there any reason why you shouldn't simply stay away? You could write her a letter saying that in consequence of her return to health, which delights you beyond measure, you propose to stop the allowance a fortnight from now. That will give her enough time to find another post if she's as good as you say. If she doesn't like it, there doesn't seem to be much she can do about it. Is there?"

There was a short pause.

"I've written a lot of silly letters," said Logan.

"Oh dear. Oh, dear me. How very unfortunate. But does it really matter?"

Logan looked at him. "I was, of course, thinking of a breach-of-promise case and all those letters being read out in court——"

"Of course you were. That's how so many women get away with it. Now let me tell you that, if what you have told me is literally true, she wouldn't have a leg to stand on. There was a time when bringing breach-of-promise actions was a lucrative side line for women; it isn't now. They have to prove that they have lost substantially in either money or reputation. For example, if she'd spent money because she was going to marry you which she wouldn't otherwise have spent—bought a house or furniture or even an expensive trousseau—you might be made to pay up."

"She hasn't," said Logan.

"Or if she had had a child——"

"Great heavens, no. I told you I meant to *marry* her. One doesn't—er——"

"Well, I'm quite sure you didn't, anyway. What makes you afraid she would bring an action? Is she vindictive by nature?"

"Oh, I shouldn't really think so," said poor Logan. "It's just that she is so very competent, I can't imagine any situation with which she couldn't cope and I was wondering how she'd cope with this one. That's all."

"Yes, I see. Get it into your head that an action for breach of promise which was merely vindictive would stand no chance at all of succeeding and no reputable solicitor would handle it. That is, if you have really given me all the relevant information."

"I'm sure I have. She's none the worse for me."

"That's the way to talk," said Fenchurch. "Now all that's worrying you is the letters, eh? Are you sure she has kept them?"

"No. But she did keep them; I mean, I know she used to store them up, she said so."

"Since you really want them—"

"I want to do this with them," said Logan, pointing to the wastepaper basket.

"Why not simply go and ask her for them?"

Logan stood up and said: "Right. I will."

"Just a moment before you rush off. You have just torn up your will; I take it you will want to make another?"

"If I get run over on the way home——"

"These things do happen," said Fenchurch, "unfortunately."

"Then the whole of my estate goes to my next of kin, doesn't it? That's my twin brother Laurence."

"That is so, yes. But the Government claims heavier death duties in the case of an intestacy. Of course it may be that you wish to give the Government a little present—no? No, then don't die intestate. Also, there were other legacies, weren't there?"

"To my secretary Miss Davie and my manservant Greene and one or two others. Yes, I see, I don't want them to be washed out. Can I come and see you one day next week and in the meantime I'll think it over?"

Fenchurch consulted an engagement calendar and said: "Will ten-thirty next Tuesday suit you?"

"Very well," said Logan, backing towards the door. "I'll be here at ten-thirty next Tuesday. Good-bye, Fenchurch."

Elizabeth Alton's flat was in a converted house in West Kensington; other tenants lived on the ground floor and the second storey, the caretaker and his wife in the basement. Logan walked up the two wide steps to the front door and rang the bell.

Nothing happened, so he rang again and yet again. Having screwed up his courage to face an interview he dreaded, exasperation seized him at being balked of it. If she was out he would wait. He opened the door—the main door of the house was only locked at night—and walked upstairs to Elizabeth Alton's own private door. It had a small brass knocker which was a model of the Imp of Lincoln. Logan knocked repeatedly, received no reply, and lost his temper. He grasped the door handle and turned it; to his surprise the door opened. She must be at home.

He put his head in and called: "Betty! Betty, are you there?" There was no answer; he went in and closed the door behind him. There was no entrance lobby; in these converted houses the doors opened straight into the sitting room and the other rooms had been made to open off that.

On the table in the middle there was a sheet of white paper, very conspicuous on the dark wood, and on it a message in Betty's neat writing: "Wait for me, I shan't be more than half an hour."

Logan's first surprised thought was to wonder how on earth she knew he was coming since he had not warned her and at this hour he was normally still at his office. Then it dawned on him that of course the message was not for him but for someone else whom she was expecting. If it were some woman friend it would be awkward being found there, and he almost turned and fled. On the other hand, if it were a man——

He laid his hat, umbrella and gloves down upon the table, walked to the window and stood looking out through the thin net curtains.

Five minutes later a man came walking fast along the street, almost running. Logan, looking down, was nearly certain that this was the same man who, on a previous occasion, had waved to Betty as he turned away.

"If he comes here——" whispered Logan.

The man came up to the front door and turned in. Logan heard the door open and shut and the sound of steps running up the stairs.

Logan picked up his hat, gloves and umbrella from the table and bolted like a rabbit into an inner room which was obviously Betty's bedroom. He looked wildly round for cover; there was a narrow built-in cupboard beside the fireplace with the door ajar. He sprang inside, crushing back dresses which hung there, and tried to pull the door shut; it would not quite close and there was no knob on the inside.

The second visitor knocked with the Lincoln Imp, waited a moment and then walked in, calling Betty's name as he did so. Then the calling stopped—he had evidently seen the note —and Logan distinctly heard him say: "Damn and blast!" in an angry voice.

After that there was silence broken only by the scrape of a match and, a little later, the smell reached him of the same strong tobacco he had smelt there before.

By this time Logan was furious with himself as well as with Betty and the man out there. What had possessed him to panic like that and hide in a dress cupboard? What a fool he would look if he were found. Logan was not the first to find that it is much easier to get into a cupboard than to emerge from it. Also his bowler hat was in his way; there was not much room and it persisted in pushing the door open, so he put it on his head. If only the man would get tired of waiting and go away.

3 *HEIRONS*

THE OUTER DOOR of the flat opened and shut and Logan heard Betty's voice. "Hello, Steve! How did the business—— What's the matter?"

The man's voice answered her, a deep voice with yet something light and reckless in its tones. "Don't get into a flap, please. There's nothing wrong that a cool head and a little ready money won't cure. I must get away, that's all."

"Steve! Is it the police again?"

Steve laughed. "Well, it's two lots actually, though it's true the police force is one of 'em. Funny thing, that, the police chasing me for something I didn't do."

"If you can prove you didn't do it, why run?"

"Oh, they know I didn't do it."

"Then why are they chasing you?"

"All these questions! Now I'll ask you one. How much money have you got?"

"None for you," said Elizabeth Alton in tones so incisive that Logan could almost see their shape cut in the air. "I've given you money and lent you money—it's the same thing, since you never pay back—and I'm sick of it." The man said something which Logan did not catch but which seemed to infuriate Betty.

"Don't you dare to quote Mother to me again! Yes, I know she left you in my charge, don't I know it! As soon as I'd left school I was working to educate you, then working to help keep you when you got your first job——"

"You got the job, I didn't," interrupted Steve. "You made me into a grubby little office boy ordered about by every——"

"You could have worked up," she said. "I had to. Then you ran away to sea and I had to pay for those binoculars you stole in Cardiff. I wouldn't pay that time you got mixed up with that forged money——"

"Nobody asked you to—Borstal and no option——"

"Then the war broke out and I did think you'd go straight. You couldn't go straight if you were walking down a passage three feet wide. You've ruined my life; I can't have any decent friends, I can't save, I can't marry the man I want to marry, I won't connect a decent man with a jailbird, and if our mother could see you she'd haunt you and serve you right!"

There was a momentary pause during which the implications of "our mother" dawned upon Logan, but before he had time to begin to rejoice Stephen Alton gave him something else to think about.

"So you're going to brush off your little brother for good and all, are you? Not just yet, you're not. It would be so unrefined, would it not"—he mimicked Betty's precise enunciation—"to have a brother tried for murder?"

Silence fell like a dropped curtain; it seemed to Logan that even his heart had stopped beating.

"Don't sit there opening and shutting your mouth like that," said Stephen Alton, "you look like a goldfish with the gapes. Who? Oh, nobody we know, only three policemen."

"*Three policemen?*"

"Yes, and I didn't shoot them, but I might be accused of complicity. You see, they'd just arrested me."

"Stop, stop!" cried Betty. "Listen. You will begin at the beginning and tell me the story plainly and truthfully, or I will ring up the police and give you in charge. I mean it. Now then."

"Oh, very well. I told you some time ago I'd got a scheme on which would net us pots of money and we could go to America and start a new life. I got hold of some drawings of something frightfully hush-hush which the German scientists in Russia had invented for the Russians. The fellow mainly responsible got out of Russia somehow, I don't know how—nor care—bringing them with him. I got hold of them—I'll tell you how some other time—and I'm selling them to the Russians. They are anxious to buy them back, naturally, and the figure, my dear Betty, is half a million sterling. So I arranged to meet a man this afternoon but I was a bit early, he wasn't in, so I said I'd come back later. On my way down the stairs from his office I met a couple of C.I.D. men. They were waiting for me, actually, wanted to pin some dock robberies onto me, or some such nonsense. So we all came downstairs together, me in the middle and the two dicks one on each side. There was a sort of entrance hall inside the front door. As we started down the last flight three men came into the hall; it was open to the public, you see, the place was a block of offices actually——"

"Get on!"

"I am getting on. I recognized one of the three, he'd been tailing me around, he was a Russian, I knew that. They were the men I was going to meet. He and the other two pulled out revolvers and loosed off with 'em, a regular fusillade, and hit both the dicks with me; why I didn't stop one too I can't think. We all fell down the stairs together amid screams from adjoining offices and one hell of an uproar, and a policeman in uniform came dashing in from the street, so my noble and gallant allies shot him too. Very violent, these Mongols. I picked myself up while the cop was falling, if you get the picture, and made one jump for the door. Outside there was a police car with the door hanging open—that was where the cop came from, he was the driver—so I hopped in and drove rapidly away. I thought it best. When I'd put quite a distance between me and the scene of slaughter I left the car in a quiet street and came on here. That's all. Oh dear——"

"Steve! What—is it your heart again?"

"Only bumping a bit," gasped Steve. "Don't fuss, for goodness' sake."

"I wish you'd see a doctor," said Betty in an anxious voice.

"Doctor nothing! Got any brandy?"

"No, but I'll get some in a——"

"Sit still!"

There was a short silence during which Logan could hear nothing, then Stephen Alton's voice came again, a little less resonant than before but still determined and incisive.

"There you are. Better already. Smoking too much, must cut it down. Funny, I never get an attack when things are really exciting, it's only after it's all over—what were we saying?"

"Hadn't you better lie down for a bit? Lie down on my bed, perhaps you'll sleep for——"

Logan was so horrified by this suggestion that he nearly had a heart attack himself. If they were to come in and find him in the cupboard, having overheard everything, that man would certainly assault him with violence and possibly kill him. But Alton's next words relieved him.

"Don't be so soppy! I'm all right now. About those Russians, wasn't it?"

Betty evidently pulled herself together. "Yes," she said. "Why did the Russians, or whoever they were, shoot the policemen? Surely they must know they will be hunted down for it?"

"Either they meant to shoot me too and take the doings off my dead body or they thought I was going willingly to hand over the doings to the British Government and they didn't approve, or they may even have grasped the fact that I was being arrested and proposed to arrest me themselves. You can believe whichever you like, I didn't wait to ask them."

"I still think you'd be much safer in the hands of the police. You didn't shoot them."

"Safer! My good, worthy elder sister, when has safety ever appealed to me? Can't you get it into your head that I've still got those designs and I'm going to get the money for them? All I want to do is to lie low till the police have caught the Russians—no one ever murders police in this country and gets away with it—and then I'll bob up again and do the deal. These damn' Russkis are an infernal nuisance, they've been trailing me everywhere I go for the past fortnight, in case I double-cross them, I suppose. You know, they're such twisters themselves they can't trust anybody else. It's very difficult to deal with people like that."

There was a prolonged pause; evidently Betty was thinking over the story and Stephen thought it wiser to let her do so undisturbed. Logan, still in the dress cupboard, felt his mind spinning. He had done Betty a series of injustices in his thoughts, that was plain, but if marrying her meant being connected with this appalling Steve he felt less inclined to it than ever.

"What I don't understand," said Betty slowly, "is how those detectives knew you were going to that office this afternoon. You said they were waiting for you."

When Alton came ashore that afternoon in Wapping he went straight to the boardinghouse at the back of Liverpool Street Station where he had a room. It was not at all a nice boardinghouse but it suited Alton since all the boarders were men, and not the sort of men to ask awkward questions. They themselves would not have liked to be asked questions. Do as you would be done by.

He called down the basement stairs to his landlady to tell her that he had come back, and ran upstairs to his own bedroom on the first floor where he shut his door and locked it. He then undressed sufficiently to get poor Muntz's packet out from where it had lain hidden between his shirt and vest and been quite remarkably uncomfortable. Alton opened the packet, spread the sheets out upon the floor and looked at them while he changed into his shore clothes.

There were seven sheets altogether, of large size, about three feet by two feet six inches. They were very beautifully drawn in jet-black Indian ink by a man who knew his work; there were copious annotations in German which conveyed nothing to Alton and they were plainly originals. Alton postponed tying his tie to examine them closely; he could see in places the original pencilling under the ink lines. He was neither a trained engineer nor an explosives expert and frankly admitted to himself that the drawings were completely incomprehensible to him. He did grasp, however, that one of them was a General Arrangement and the others details of the parts shown in outline.

He finished dressing and sat down on his bed to smoke a cigarette, still looking doubtfully at the plans on the floor They were doubtless very beautiful to anyone who liked that kind of thing and, he hoped, immensely valuable, but how horribly large and bulky. Fancy trying to conceal those things where nobody could find them; you might as well try to conceal the Sailing Directions. Well, nearly.

He stubbed out that cigarette, lit another, and lay back on his bed staring at the ceiling and thinking. A quarter of an hour later he got up, packed up the sheets again and went out with them to see a friend of his.

He returned later so pleased with himself that he rang up his sister and took her out to dinner. It was then that he told her that he was on to something which would make both their fortunes, though he did not tell her then what it was. He was not consciously fond of his sister and he alternately raged and sneered when she tried to reform him, but whenever anything either good or bad happened to him some quite irresistible power compelled him to go and tell her about it. The compulsion infuriated him but he went all the same, and what is more, he always told her the truth if not the whole truth. She was twelve years older than he was and all the mother he had ever known.

The next move was to get in touch with the Russians. It was safe to assume that Russia had already found out that their precious design for death was no longer within their borders, or if they hadn't they soon would. When they came to enquire they would probably discover which way their truant expert had fled and where he was making for. After all, where would a truant expert escaping from Russia make for? England, of course, if only en route to the United States. In due course, therefore, pursuant Russians might be expected in London.

Alton let a few days pass and then went to see Ernie Heirons, with whom he had done business before. Heirons was not exactly what is meant by a "fence," although he did not mind receiving stolen goods. He had a quite remarkable gift for finding someone who wanted to buy whatever somebody else wanted to sell. He never handled the goods himself; all he did was to find a buyer for any seller, arrange the terms and take his percentage. He would sell anything from a diamond necklace to a live wart hog with measles, but he never handled either the diamonds or the hog. He had helped Alton to dispose of a lot of miscellaneous items which were listed missing from the London Docks. He was a short fat man with a squint and he never uttered one word more than was necessary.

"I've got a little job for you," said Atlon, "though I don't know when it will come off. Perhaps not for weeks."

Heirons looked at him and away again and Alton said that Russia had lost some plans and might be expected to make enquiry for them in London. Could Heirons get to know if and when any such enquiry were made? They—the Russians —would probably start asking questions in the underworld of London and no doubt Heirons could hear of it through his contacts.

Heirons continued to stare fixedly at his inkpot for some moments after Alton had finished speaking and eventually said: "Don't like it."

"Don't like what?"

"Russians."

"Oh, nonsense," said Alton. "Why not? They want to buy, we want to sell. What's the matter? They're men like anybody else, aren't they?"

"No," said Heirons.

"Look here, Ernie," said Alton, and reasoned with him at some length until eventually Heirons nodded his head unwillingly. It was the mention of half a million sterling which did it. Even a small percentage of half a million is what anybody would call money, and Heiron's percentage was not small.

"I want the money in dollars," said Alton, "paid into an

account in my name in a bank in New York. I'm leaving this country. I'm tired of a place where the police——"

"Go away," said Heirons, and Alton went.

It was nearly seven weeks before Alton had any news about Russians and then Heirons sent for him to tell him that there were three citizens of the Soviet Union, living on a small Polish ship lying near Tower Bridge, who were asking about missing plans in a manner so excessively guarded that it was very difficult to know what, if anything, they were talking about. However, if one guessed what they were trying to say, it was possible to perceive that they were trying to say it. If Alton was still interested Heirons would get into contact with them.

"Still interested?" said Alton. "What, in half a million? What d'you take me for?"

"A fool," said Heirons.

"Don't take that tone with me," snapped Alton. "Why d'you say it, anyway?"

"Won't pay."

"Then they won't get them and I'll go to the British Government instead."

Heirons merely looked at him and then, pointedly, at the door. Alton went, fuming, but he could not afford to quarrel with Heirons, there was nobody like him.

On the same afternoon as that on which Edward Logan went to see his solicitor, Alton had an appointment in Heirons' office at half-past three to meet the Russians and discuss terms. He went at a quarter past, he wanted to see Heirons before the Russians arrived, but the "mercantile agent," as he called himself, was out and his clerk did not know when he would come back. "There is plenty of time, Mr. Alton. It is you who are too early."

"I know," said Alton. "I wanted to see him."

He fidgeted about the office for some five minutes and then said that he would go for a stroll and come back later.

Alton had not spent in idleness his seven weeks of waiting for the Russians. Robberies from the London Docks had continued, culminating in a particularly daring raid upon a bonded warehouse stored with whisky for export to happier lands. This time Alton had done what the Wapping police sergeant had foretold: he had slipped up and somebody had been induced to talk about it. On the morning of the meeting at Heirons' office word had gone out that Alton, if seen, was to be reported at once; photographs and a description accompanied the word. When, therefore, a constable on his beat had seen Alton turn into Heirons' office building he hurried to the nearest police telephone box and rang up Scotland Yard who, in their turn, wirelessed the nearest patrol car. By the time the constable had returned to the interesting spot, the patrol car swept up to the door and two plain-clothes men got out.

"Is he still there?"

"So far as I know. He's only just gone in. He went upstairs."

The plain-clothes men nodded and went inside and the constable continued upon his beat. Those two men could deal with Alton.

Heirons' office was upon the second floor; Alton came out and walked down as far as the first floor. Here, upon the narrow landing, he met two men whom he hardly noticed, being lost in thought upon his own affairs. They stood back politely to let him pass, one upon either side of the way; as he came between them each of them shot out a hand and held him by either arm.

"What the devil——"

"You are Stephen Alton," said one of them. "We are taking you to the police station for questioning in connection with a robbery at the Docks."

Alton forced a laugh. "You're all wrong," he said. "I'm not Stephen whatever-you-said, and I don't know anything about the Docks."

"You can tell them all that at the station. We think you can help us."

There was nothing to be done, especially as they continued to hold his arms. They came down the lower flight of stairs abreast like close friends; as soon as Alton came within sight of the hall below he saw three men standing there as though uncertain where to go. He recognized them at once, for he had had them pointed out to him as the Russians he wanted, and he had seen them several times since. In fact, he seemed to keep on seeing them; there was no doubt but that the interest was mutual nor, also, that someone had pointed him out to them, though they had never made the slightest attempt to speak to him.

Alton, still on the stairs, hung back momentarily and it became obvious that he was being officially escorted. The Russians' eyes widened, one said something to the others and the next moment their guns were out and they were firing up the stairs.

The detective on Alton's left coughed suddenly, let go of

his prisoner's arm and pitched headfirst down the stairs; the one on his right clutched at Alton with both hands as though determined not to lose him, and they rolled down the last half-dozen steps together. Before they had come to rest at the bottom pandemonium had broken out in the offices, doors opened on all sides and heads poked out of them or appeared over the banisters above accompanied by feminine screams and masculine curses. The Russians seemed to be a little disconcerted by this violent reaction to what no doubt appeared to them a simple and even laudable action; they drew together and lowered their guns while Alton shook himself free of the clinging detective and scrambled to his feet. From the two office doors nearest the street bold men dashed out to call in the constable who was usually thereabouts; in the outer doorway they collided with the uniformed driver of the police car who was rushing in. Alton seized the moment of confusion to bolt out at the door; as he leapt for it the fusillade broke out again and one bullet which missed the policeman whistled past Alton's ear into the doorpost.

Just across the narrow pavement the police car was standing with the door open; Alton threw himself into the driver's seat and attempted to drive away. The make of car—a Vauxhall—was unfamiliar to him and he was not a motorist of much experience. He started the engine, put the car into the wrong gear and let in the clutch; the engine naturally stopped again. Frantic with haste, he tried again and was more successful this time; the car moved off, gathered speed and was lost to sight round the next corner.

He did not notice a grey car which came out from a cul-de-sac next to Heirons' office and settled down to follow him. He turned and twisted through the streets, keeping in the general direction of West Kensington; when he was within easy walking distance of Betty's flat he abandoned the car and finished his journey on foot.

The grey car pulled up behind the police car. Its passengers appeared to be holding a conference.

4 | HALF A MILLION DOLLARS

"I DON'T KNOW how the police knew I was going to Heirons' office this afternoon," said Stephen Alton slowly. "I haven't had time to think it out. Now you mention it, Betty, it is a bit odd. I wonder if——"

Logan, still hidden in the clothes closet, heard the outer door of the flat open; there was a loud exclamation from Alton and a short scream from Betty. Then a new voice with a tone of command: "Put up your hands!"

"Oh dear," said Logan half aloud, "oh dear, I hope this is the police; oh dear, what the hell possessed me to come here——"

"Madam," said the same voice, doubtless addressing Betty, "be so good as to go and sit in that chair against the wall, be quiet and keep still. *Quieta non movere*, if you have had the benefit of a classical education." The voice was smooth, almost pleasant, and with only a hint of a foreign accent under the correct English.

"Not the police," whispered Logan.

"Now, Mr. Stephen Alton, where are those designs which I understand you have for sale?"

"Where you won't find them," said Alton, and Logan noticed with unwilling admiration that his voice had not changed in the least, it was still careless and confident. "So it's no use your looking for them. When you have paid half a million sterling, in dollars, into a New York bank in my name, I will give them to you without any of this silly gun play."

"Half a million pounds is a lot of money," said the Russian.

"They're worth more than that to you."

"Let us not haggle. You will hand over the designs to me now and we will reward you richly."

"What's your offer?"

"You are a young man, Mr. Alton. Shall we say forty or fifty years of life? A rich reward indeed; what money could buy it? A paltry half million?"

"What are you getting at?"

"Your life, Mr. Alton, your life," said the Russian, and his smooth voice became rasping. "Hand over those drawings and you shall live. If not——"

"If I die you'll never see them," said Alton calmly, "for I'm the only person who knows where they are."

"To die is not so simple, nor so quick. I was not thinking of a bullet through the head. You shall pray for a bullet through the head."

Betty cried out suddenly, "Oh, this is dreadful, dreadful," and burst into loud sobbing.

"There, you see," said the Russian, "you upset your wife, your poor wife who loves you. Consider your poor wife."

"—my 'poor wife,'" said Alton.

"I am tired of this," said the Russian suddenly. "Search him, Piotr. If the papers are not on him we will look further. They are not so small, these plans, it is not easy to hide so large a packet."

Alton's expression did not change; one of the Russians held a gun close to his ear while another ran his hands over his body. It was plain at once that Alton was not carrying on his person any packet of anything like the size of Muntz's original parcel, and the search of the flat began. Logan could hear cupboard doors being opened and the contents pulled out, sometimes with the crash of breaking glass and china. Betty began a loud protest but was snarled into silence. Drawers were pulled right out and overturned on the floor, her two padded armchairs were slashed and the carpet dragged up. The sitting room having yielded nothing, two of the Russians came into the bedroom while the third still stood guard over Alton.

When they flung open the door of the clothes closet Logan drew himself up and stepped out: tall, stern and stately with his bowler hat still upon his head because he had forgotten it was there, his neat umbrella hanging by its crook handle upon his arm and his dark grey suède gloves held firmly in his hand. The Russians uttered loud exclamations of surprise and all three turned to watch Alton's face as Logan stalked past them into the sitting room; their eyebrows went up when they saw that his only reaction was definitely amusement. As Logan came through the doorway Betty looked round and saw him, gave a faint shriek and fainted.

Two of the Russians looked on unmoved but the third doubled up with laughter. He clung to the doorpost, indicated Betty, Alton and Logan with a significant triangular gesture and laughed till the tears rolled down his face. Logan reddened to the hair with anger and embarrassment and dropped into the nearest chair; indeed, his knees were giving way.

The Russians finished searching the bedroom and left it in the same state of chaos as the sitting room; the small kitchen and the bathroom did not detain them long.

"They are not here," said the spokesman. "This is your last chance. Where are they?"

"I told you you wouldn't find them," said Alton contemptuously. "Now will you talk sense? Pay up, and you shall have them."

The Russians consulted together in their own language; Logan, irritated and frightened, craved for a smoke. Lying on the table beside him was a cigarette case; actually it was Stephen Alton's and not his own, but Logan was too preoccupied to notice. He took out a cigarette, lit it at Betty's table lighter which he himself had given her, and unconsciously dropped the case into his own pocket. Betty began to regain consciousness, moving her head and moaning quietly, but no one took any notice of her.

One of the Russians indicated Logan and said something, another seized Logan by the arm, jerked him to his feet and ran quick hands over him as they had done with Alton.

"I protest——" began Logan indignantly, but the Russian who had done all the talking interrupted him.

"Our heartfelt apologies," he said blandly. "We do of course realize—we are men of the world—your interest in this household is not so prosaic as——"

"Damn you, sir," roared Logan, losing his temper completely, "keep your filthy insinuations to yourself!"

"Your interest in this household," said the Russian, tapping him on the chest, "had better be romantic. Exclusively romantic, do you understand? You will find it safer. Much safer. It—is—not—at—all—safe to play with us," emphasizing each word with a jab from a hard finger; "as you say in England, 'If you can't be good, be careful!'" He turned sharply upon Alton, and his tone changed. "You will come with us. One unguarded move, the slightest attempt to escape or attract attention, and I will empty this gun into your body. Remember those policemen? Now, out of the door."

Alton went; he had no choice with a gun in his ribs. They went down the stairs to the front door, Logan staggered to the window and saw them all get into the grey saloon car, which was immediately driven away.

Betty Alton came out of her faint and sat up, shivering miserably, with tears running down her face. Logan was touched with pity; if he had had an ugly hour, what must it have been for her?

"It's all right now," he said gently, "they've all gone away now. I'll lock the outer door," and he did so.

"Steve—my brother—they took him away? Oh, what will they do to him?"

"So far as I can see, that rests with him, m'dear. I gather that he has something they want. Very well. He has only to give it to them and all will be well. Besides, it appears that these are the men who shot three policemen earlier this afternoon in broad daylight in a busy office. Their descriptions will have been circulated all over London by now; they cannot long escape arrest if they haven't been stopped already. I think you should ring up the police and tell them that these Russians have just left here——"

"I can't do that."

"Why not?"

"Because—I don't know how much you heard—the police are after Steve too."

Logan shrugged his shoulders. All this was emphatically no business of his and he was quite determined that it should never become his business. Those dreadful men; suppose Alton would not give them whatever it was, suppose they evaded arrest, they might come back and look for him instead—— He would go away, he would go abroad now, at once, tonight, he would go to Laurence in Paris, Laurence was the man to deal with this kind of thing. He liked excitement and doubtful company and battles of wits in several languages. Odd, thought Edward Logan as he usually did when he thought of his brother, odd that identical twins, born within twenty minutes, and with the same upbringing, should be so alike in outward appearance and so totally different in every other respect. He pulled himself together; this was a moment for action, not meditation.

Betty was moving feebly round the room picking up things from the floor and putting them aimlessly somewhere else. There was one unbroken out of a set of four Crown Derby cups which she cherished; the Russians had merely swept them off the cupboard shelf. She picked up the unbroken one; it slipped from uncertain fingers to the boards and smashed into a dozen pieces. Elizabeth Alton, that calm competent woman, burst into floods of tears, rushed into her bedroom, slammed the door and locked it.

Logan hardly noticed her going; the first thing to do was to ring up Laurence in Paris, and there was no knowing how long the call would take. Better telephone from here at once.

He sat down by the telephone and gave the operator a Paris number. "Will it be long coming through?" The operator said he couldn't promise, the lines were pretty clear this side but there was no telling what they were like once you got abroad. Logan gave him Betty's number and told him to ring back when the connection was made. "In the meantime I've got one or two local calls to make."

Logan rang up his office and told Miss Davie that he had to go to Paris unexpectedly on urgent business and might be away three or four days. He would write to her from Paris. In the meantime she could carry on. Anything requiring his personal attention must stand over till his return. Nancy Davie made all the correct answers until Logan hung up the receiver; if she hummed *"Sous les toits de Paris"* after that it did not matter since he could not hear her.

Logan rang up his own flat and his manservant answered the call.

"Greene, this is Mr. Logan. I have to go unexpectedly to Paris tonight by the night ferry service to Dunkirk. Will you pack two bags with all I shall need for four or five days and meet me with the luggage at Victoria just after nine o'clock? I shall want my passport too; it is in the second drawer of the mahogany bureau, on the left-hand side. In the same drawer on the right-hand side there is a bank envelope with fifteen one-pound notes in it. Bring me five of them, please, only five. Buy a second-class return to Paris and a sleeping-car reservation. Is that clear? Luggage, passport, five pounds and my ticket and reservation at Victoria just after nine tonight."

He hung up again and looked anxiously at the telephone. If the call were too slow those horrible men might come back, they might be on their way even now, they might arrive at any moment. All this waiting—he was not really nervous, of course not, but waiting for something unpleasant was a thing to unman the brav——

The telephone bell rang; he started violently and snatched up the receiver, relieved beyond measure to hear his brother's voice at the other end.

"That you, Laurence, thank goodness. Listen, I'm coming over tonight by the Dunkirk ferry; will you meet me at the Gare du Nord in the morning?"

Laurence's voice, cool and faintly mocking: "This is very sudden, brother Edward, you generally give me about six weeks' notice of your rare visits. Still, glad to see you; certainly I'll meet the train. Twenty past nine tomorrow morning."

"Oh, Laurence. Would you please book a room for me. Usual hotel, the D'Amboise."

"Certainly. Oh no, by the way, the D'Amboise is closed for redecoration, I passed it yesterday. I'll get you a room at the St. Pétersbourg in the Rue Caumartin. Lots of English go there, you'll like it."

Edward Logan repeated the name and address. "But are you sure they'll have a room? I must leave my address with Greene."

"I'm not sure, of course, but I expect so. I'll ring up and ask them and ring you back; where are you, at your flat?"

"No—no, I'm not. And I can't wait, Laurence. I—I don't want to stay in this place a minute longer than I can help."

"Edward, Edward, what haunt of vice have you strayed into and——"

"I'm not joking and it isn't funny. I am in great danger, my life is threatened. If I can but catch that train I'll tell you all about it—I want your advice."

"You shall have it. As for catching the train, you have— let me see—something over four hours in which to get to Victoria. You ought to manage it quite easily."

"Laurence, I tell you——"

"All right, all right. Sorry I can't help pulling your leg."

"Where can I go to be safe in the meantime? I don't want to go home, they may know where I live."

"Go and have a Turkish bath. No one, so far as I know, has ever been murdered in a Turkish bath. Well, keep your tail up, old horse. See you tomorrow."

There was a click at the far end of the line; Laurence had hung up. Edward put the receiver back on its rest, stood up and looked anxiously about him. Hat, gloves, umbrella. He listened for a moment at Betty's door; there was no sound from within. Perhaps she had gone to sleep. Best thing possible, sleep. Soothing, refreshing, restorative. It would be cruel to disturb her.

Edward Logan tiptoed to the outer door, let himself out quietly and ran down the stairs. A taxi was in the act of decanting a customer at the house next door. Logan hailed it and was driven to a Turkish bath establishment in Westminster, conveniently near Victoria Station.

"Logan's got them," gasped Alton, and fell back in his chair; a thin trickle of blood was running down his left

cheek. The three men who were standing over him looked
at each other.

"Logan! Who's Logan?"

"The man you saw at the flat."

"You mean your wife's lover?"

"She's not my wife, she's my sister."

"I believe that," said the first Russian, speaking in that
language which Alton did not understand. "That is why he
looked amused when we found the man in the cupboard."
He reverted to English. "This Logan, who is he?"

"A businessman—Londoner."

"His address?"

Alton thought for a moment and gave it, a block of flats near
Regent's Park, Caroline Mansions. "I can't remember the number, but you'll find it in the telephone directory."

"His first names?"

"She called him Edward. E. J. Logan, that's it."

The three men consulted together while Alton lay back in
his chair with his eyes closed.

"It could be true, Brachko," said one. "The sister's fiancé,
he could have been in the business."

"I don't believe it," said Brachko. "They did not know
each other, they neither looked at each other nor spoke. I was
there all the time, you remember, Yudin, watching them."

"An act," said Yudin. "They put on an act. These English
are above all things deceitful."

"We searched him," objected Brachko. "He had not got
them on him."

"That is not to say they are not in his possession. He may
have had them for weeks. We can ask this man when he
gave Logan the designs. He is in a mood to answer and he
had better!"

The third man, who had been questioning Alton, objected
to this. "I am a doctor, as you know," he said. "I examined
him when we brought him here. I advise you for your own
sakes to let him rest for at least two hours. His heart is in a
really bad state and you have not improved matters. Any
sudden shock might be fatal. I am surprised that he survived
the excitement of the attack on the police this afternoon."

Yudin looked annoyed. "Can't you give him something to
keep him going, Chadai?"

"What, with a heart in that state? You cannot help being
ignorant," said the doctor loftily, "but you need not be
foolish, Yudin."

"I will just ask him that one question," said Brachko, and turned towards Alton, who started and shrank back.

"I want a cigarette," he said. "Can I have a cigarette?"

"You may," said Dr. Chadai. "Have one of ours." He turned towards a cigarette box on a shelf screwed to the cabin bulkhead, but Alton said he would rather have one of his own. Moving carefully, he slipped his right hand inside his coat as though to take out a cigarette case, but suddenly a look of incredulous horror crossed his face, he flushed scarlet, the colour ebbed away as quickly, and with one gasping breath he fell sideways in his chair.

The doctor, who had been watching him closely, sprang towards him and bent over the chair. He straightened up a moment later and turned to the others, hands in his pockets and cigarette sticking upwards from the corner of his mouth.

"It's to be hoped that you catch your Logan and that he is willing to talk. This one won't talk any more."

"Why not?"

"Because he's dead. He put his hand across his chest like this. I thought he was feeling for cigarettes but he may have been clutching his heart. Anyway, he's died as I warned you he would."

"It is as well we are on a ship on the river," said Yudin. "It is only to wait till it is dark and drop him over the side. Now we had better go and see the dignified Logan. Brachko, go ashore and ring up Cutler, tell him we want the car again at once."

Brachko nodded and went out. When he came back he said that Cutler would come as soon as possible. "He has driven the grey car away somewhere and left it. He says he will borrow another car and come as quickly as he can; he'll get one from a theatre car-park, it won't be missed till the show's over."

"He will probably be able to put it back before the owner misses it," agreed Yudin. "But why has he abandoned the grey car? I know it was stolen, but he said he had altered it so much that no one would recognize it."

"He is not afraid of its being recognized as stolen. He is afraid it will be recognized as the car which was parked near Heirons' office this afternoon and driven away after the shooting. Our chauffeur, my dear Yudin, violently disapproves of shooting policemen. He says policemen are not shot in England because, if they are, the shooter is always hung."

"Rubbish," said Yudin.

"Always, he says. When I told him that it was police who

had been shot I thought he was going to faint. He says if we shoot any more police we can find another driver."

"An English custom, doubtless," said Dr. Chadai drily. "Like not shooting foxes, you know."

"I daresay," said Brachko, "but they don't hang you for shooting foxes, do they?"

5 TRAIN FERRY

THE CAR PASSED the entrance to Caroline Mansions and Chadai got out. "I'll go and find out which floor Logan's flat is on and have a general look round. I wonder whether there is a concierge, for example: commissionaires, they call them here, don't they? Turn the car round, Cutler, and if I signal to you come up to the door."

Chadai had been the spokesman at Elizabeth Alton's flat because his English accent was the best in the party; he always took the lead for this reason whenever it was necessary to talk to the English. He walked back unhurriedly towards the entrance of Caroline Mansions, but just before he reached it a stout middle-aged man came out of the doorway carrying two suitcases which he set down upon the edge of the pavement. They were expensive-looking leather suitcases and bore their owner's name neatly stamped upon the lid: E. J. Logan. The time was a quarter to nine and Logan's manservant Greene was carrying out his instructions. Chadai passed the entrance and paused to tie up his shoelace as the commissionaire came out.

"Shall I ring for a taxi?" he asked, but Greene said he need not bother, there would be one along in a minute. "There's plenty of time," he added. "I've only got to buy his ticket; the train don't go for an hour yet."

"Sudden trip this time, isn't it?"

"In business," said Greene a little stiffly, "we never know."

"No, I don't suppose so," said the commissionaire, and went indoors again. Chadai straightened himself and went back to the waiting car.

"He's going off somewhere," he said. "Cutler, when a taxi

picks up that man, follow and don't lose it on any account."

"I'll do me best," said Cutler surlily, "but you don't get me running down no policemen, not just to chase a blinking taxi."

"My good Cutler," said Chadai, "you have policemen on the brain."

"Ah, I 'ave," agreed Cutler, "and for why? 'Cause I'd rather 'ave cops on the brain than a noose round me neck. You're foreigners, you don't understand."

"You will do what you are ordered to do," said Yudin peremptorily.

"I'll do what I see fit to do," said Cutler angrily. "I'm not your slave. An' I tells you point blank, if those cops this afternoon 'ad been dead, you wouldn't 'ave seen me tonight. No, nor ever again."

"Aren't they dead, then?" asked Yudin indifferently.

"No. Two's in 'ospital, t'other weren't much 'urt; it's in the evenin' paper what I——"

"There's a taxi," interrupted Chadai. "Now."

A taxi drew up at Caroline Mansions, received Greene and the luggage, turned in the road and went off; Cutler followed it. There were some anxious moments at traffic lights and road junctions but they managed to keep the taxi in sight until it turned into the station yard at Victoria and the car followed closely. In the yard the three Russians, Yudin, Brachko and Dr. Chadai, got out; almost before they were clear of the car Cutler slammed the door and drove hastily away.

Logan's manservant was within a few yards of them, paying off his taxi. Chadai indicated him with a glance and the Russians strolled past him towards the station entrance. A moment later he overtook them and they fell in behind.

Greene led the way to the Continental booking office and asked for a second-class return to Paris. "Where do I book a sleeper?"

"Along there and round to the right."

Again the Russians followed. "Paris," said Yudin in a low tone. "Have you got your passport on you, Brachko?"

"Of course."

"Good, so have I. We may have to go to Paris."

Brachko nodded. "It will be pleasant, I like Paris."

The place where sleepers are booked is a brightly lighted room with a long counter, in general arrangement exactly like a bar only with clerks instead of bartenders and not a bottle in sight.

"It would be helpful," said the Russian doctor, "if you knew whereabouts in the train he is travelling."

"You are right, Chadai," said Yudin.

Chadai went in through the glass-panelled doors; there was only one clerk on duty at that time and the Russian waited while he gave Greene the sleeping-car reservation for which he asked.

"There you are," said the clerk. "B 14. You'll have a compartment all to yourself tonight, there aren't many people travelling."

"Thank you, that will be very nice," said Greene. He paid for the reservation and walked out; the clerk turned to the Russian. Chadai asked what time the night-ferry train left, and was told it was twenty-two hours, 10 P.M. English time. He thanked the clerk and went outside.

"The train is half empty," said Chadai to Yudin. "He has a compartment to himself, number B 14. That will be a two-berth compartment numbered thirteen and fourteen; if you could get the one next door, eleven and twelve, it would be a help."

Yudin nodded. "It is necessary to get the tickets first."

"Should we not get them now?" asked Brachko.

"Not yet," said Chadai. "We'll make sure first that he is really going."

"But, even if he does go, how do you know that he will have the stuff on him? If I were in his place I would put it in a bank and——"

"I don't know, of course. But banks close at fifteen hours in this country; we know Alton didn't go to a bank between Heirons' office and his sister's place, and it was too late after that."

"They hadn't got it on them at the flat," objected Brachko.

"We didn't search the woman," said Chadai.

"Why didn't we?"

"Because she'd have screamed the place down, and all the windows were open, didn't you notice?"

"Oh well," said Brachko. "But I still don't understand why you expect to find it on him."

"Fool," said Yudin wearily, "he may have it or he may not, but we have got to make sure. Even you must see that. If he hasn't got it we come back to London, that's all."

They were standing back in the angle of a bookstall, holding unlit cigarettes in their fingers for which Chadai had his lighter ready; Logan might pass them at any moment now. "Be very careful," said Chadai, "not to let him see your face. If he recognizes us he'll yell for the police."

The time dragged on to the half-hour when, just as Brachko

was saying that Logan was not coming, he came in haste and passed close by them. Greene saw him coming and raised his hand; Logan hurried to meet him, looking neither to right nor left. They met, Greene signalled a porter to take the luggage and could be seen giving Logan the tickets. It was enough.

"You wait here," said Yudin, "and watch. He will pass that barrier on the left if he's going. I'll go and get the tickets."

Logan had loitered in his Turkish bath until almost the half-hour and then made a rush for the station. Once inside, among throngs of people and under bright lights, he felt more confident; convinced that danger threatened him only in London, his spirits rose as he saw the familiar barricades, the long slippery Customs bench and the end coaches of the Paris train. Once aboard the train he would be quite safe, once in France safer still, and then in Paris Laurence could take over. He took the tickets from Greene and approved the arrangements.

"Thank you, Greene, thank you. I'll let you know when I'm coming back. Three or four days, probably."

"This way, sir," said the porter, taking his suitcases. "Customs first and then Currency Control. This way."

"Good-bye, Greene."

"Good-bye, sir. I hope you have a good crossing."

Logan smiled, nodded and hurried after the porter. He was out of sight before Yudin came back with the tickets.

"Now for the reservations. Brachko, you'd better come in with me. Chadai, you'll wait?"

The doctor nodded and the other two went into the office.

"Two sleeping-car reservations, please, on tonight's train. Is it going to be very full?"

"No, sir, very empty. Would you—are you two gentlemen travelling together?—would you like separate compartments?"

"No, thanks," said Yudin, "I don't think so. We're used to travelling together."

The clerk nodded and began turning over some small sheets clipped together. "B," he murmured, "C."

"Ah, B," said Yudin with a laugh. "Since you say the train is so empty, you have not by chance got B 11 and 12 available?"

The clerk smiled politely; he spent his days listening to travellers' odd fancies. "We have, sir, as it happens. Would you like that one?"

"Please. It is an odd coincidence, but the last twice I went to Paris on this train I had that compartment and I did very well on arrival—my business, you know. It is perhaps lucky."

"Possibly, sir," said the clerk, filling up the flimsy blue tickets. "At least it is not thirteen."

"Ah," said Yudin gravely, "the unlucky number. No, I should not want that."

Brachko uttered a strangled snort, Yudin trod on his foot and apologized. They went outside and found Chadai waiting; Brachko was spluttering with laughter which ran on into one of his long infectious peals as soon as they were beyond the clerk's hearing.

"What's amusing you?" asked the doctor.

"He's—he's got thirteen——" gurgled Brachko.

"Thirteen what?"

"Thirteen dead tomcats," snarled Yudin.

"No, no, Logan's seat num——"

"Fool," said Chadai savagely. "Now, how much English money have you got? You can only take five pounds. Give me the rest. You have plenty of francs."

They did so quickly and hurried off towards the barrier. Chadai turned on his heel and went out of the station.

"I suppose," said Brachko anxiously, "that that is quite safe? Giving Dr. Chadai all that money?"

"Are you suggesting that Dr. Chadai will make off with it?"

"No—oh no, no. What a dreadful thing to suggest. No, I only thought he might get run over and killed, or be arrested These things do happen, Yudin."

"Tickets, please," said the collector at the gate. "To the left, please, for Customs and Currency Control. Tickets, please."

Brachko hung back behind Yudin.

"What's the matter?"

"Only making sure Logan has gone on out of sight."

"Of course, he's out of sight ten minutes ago. Yes, messieurs," to the Customs men—"we have no luggage. We are but going to Paris for tomorrow and back tomorrow night. A hurried trip, as you say, a hurried trip. This business, what it gives us of trouble. Yes, here are our passports."

Yudin produced two perfectly good French passports which resembled their holders sufficiently nearly except that the names upon them were not Yudin and Brachko. "We are French, as you see, messieurs. We are going home."

They were passed on to Currency Control, one man sitting at a folding table; behind him stands a member of the Security Police whose duty it is to look people over and make sure that they are not wanted for home consumption in the maw of Justice. If the Russians had realized that such a man would be standing just there they might have abandoned their journey though actually they had nothing to fear. The police, desiring at Heirons' office descriptions of the gunmen, had been offered word pictures which would have fitted anyone from Boris Karloff to the Hunchback of Notre Dame. In point of fact Dr. Chadai was dignified and composed and Brachko was small, furtive and inconspicuous; only the tall Yudin looked coldly dangerous.

Yudin and Brachko brazened it out since there was no help for it. The Currency Control officer held out his hand for their passports. "You are travelling to France? You know that you are not allowed to take more than five pounds each in British Treasury notes? How much English money have you, please?"

"Five pounds," said Yudin, showing it, "and some odd silver." He took a handful of small change out of his pocket. "Seven and six—oh, less than ten shillings."

"That is quite in order, thank you. Have you any foreign currency?"

Yudin took out a wallet and opened it. "Five—nearly six thousand French francs. That is all, m'sieu."

"Thank you. You know, do you, that you are not allowed to spend your English money abroad? It is for use on British ships only or for travelling expenses and Customs duties on your return."

"I understand," said Yudin, and made way for Brachko, who also satisfied the Control officer. They passed on together and emerged on the platform where the Paris train stood waiting.

"I have only just realized what a frightful risk we are now running," said Brachko. "He is in that train before us, or perhaps he is standing on the platform talking to a friend. He has only to glance round, or look out of his window, or come into the corridor just as we have entered it and we are lost. He will call the police and we shall be arrested——"

"If you're not careful," said Yudin, turning sharply upon him, "you'll find yourself being sent back to Russia, proved incompetent. You know what that means, don't you? What's the matter with you?"

"I don't like this country," said Brachko. "I know the people are all stupid bourgeoisie, but—I shall be all right when we are again in France.'

"You'd better be. As for his seeing us, he won't. He is not on the platform; look, there is carriage B. That tall man, is he there? No. He is in his compartment, unpacking. I shall take one small precaution only." He pulled down his hatbrim, turned up his collar and put on a pair of smoked glasses. "That will do. You can make what arrangements you please."

Brachko decided to have a bad cold. He retired behind a large coloured handkerchief, blowing his nose and coughing hollowly. They walked along the platform and up the steps into the coach marked B, where they were met by the conductor in charge of it. He led them along the corridor to their compartment, showed them in and said he hoped that they would be comfortable. He would take their passports and tickets now, please, as they had to be shown at Dover and Dunkirk. It would save disturbing the gentlemen again that night. He would bring them back again in the morning in good time before reaching Paris.

"Then," said Brachko, "are we not visited for any purpose at all during the night?" They were speaking French, since the train staff on the Dunkirk ferry are all Frenchmen. Brachko was much more fluent in French than in English.

"Not at all; m'sieu can sleep undisturbed all the way to Paris. If you wish me to come you have only to press that bell."

In the compartment next door Logan had unpacked what he wanted for the night and was getting into his pyjamas before the journey started. It is easier to undress before the train starts rocking. Since he was alone in the compartment he had the spare bunk on which to spread out his things; when he emptied the pockets of the suit he was wearing he found the cigarette case he picked up in Betty's flat.

It puzzled him for a moment, he could not imagine from whence it had come; he opened it and saw engraved inside the two words: "From Betty." With that, recollection returned of taking it from the table and smoking one of the cigarettes it contained; a nasty cigarette, he had not enjoyed it, but at the time everything had been so supremely horrible that it had seemed only natural that even cigarettes should have caught the general contagion. He looked at the cigarettes left in it; he himself always smoked a good Virginian if any, he was not a heavy smoker. This case no doubt belonged to Betty's brother; she should have it back when he returned to London. He dropped the cigarette case into his open suitcase.

The train started smoothly and Logan hung up his suit in the blue enamelled wardrobe. All the fittings and cupboards were enamelled blue in the second-class coaches and Logan admired it. He washed his hands in the little handbasin, drew the blind aside for a moment to watch the lights of Bromley sliding past, and then climbed into his bunk, tucked himself in, and settled down with a book. The light was in his eyes but, after a careful study of an embarrassing array of knobs and switches, he managed to turn on the bed light and turn off the others. He would read for a little and then go to sleep, he could always sleep in a train. It would be agreeable to sleep throughout the Channel crossing; he had always crossed by day before, by the Golden Arrow, and never quite enjoyed the Channel.

He was tired, overexcited and fidgety, sleep would not come. He fell asleep just before they reached Dover and was awakened again by the train stopping, being shunted, stopping again. There was a slight sensation of floating; they must be on the ship and he was wide awake. He drew up his blind and looked out; there were men attaching strong chains between the side of the coach and a sort of little platform. Then there were screwing noises and the coach lifted and steadied. Large jacks are placed under the sleeping cars and screwed up to put the springs out of action, otherwise the motion of the sea would be greatly accentuated. "If I hadn't undressed," he thought, "I could go out and see just what they are doing." He yawned suddenly, lost interest, and climbed back into bed.

He was awakened again by the train being shunted once more; he sat up, pulled aside the blind, and looked out. There was no moon but the scene was illuminated by arc lamps high and lonely on tall standards; there were many railway lines and beyond them the sterile unevenness which marks the site of bombed houses. There was a road with men cycling along it to work—what an hour to start, five in the morning—and, somewhere in the background, a ship.

"Dunkirk," he said. "So I slept soundly all the way across. Good."

He went to sleep again at once and had no idea what the time was when he was once more awakened by a steady persistent tapping at his locked door. He sat up dazedly, switched on the light and said irritably: "Well? What is it?"

A deprecating voice outside said that it was desolated to disturb monsieur but they had now cleared Dunkirk and, his passport being no longer required, it was now being returned, please.

"Go away," said Logan, and amended it to "*Allez-en. Je ne le*—I don't want it now. Keep it till we get to Paris. *Retenez-le enfin*——" He forgot the word for "until" and started again. "*Retournez-le à moi au temps que nous venons à Paris.*"

"*Pardon, m'sieu?*"

"*A Paris, seulement.*"

The voice outside said certainly, monsieur, the train only went to Paris and would monsieur have the infinite goodness to unlock his door and receive his passport?

"*Je ne veux que sommelier*," roared Logan, intending to say that he only wanted to sleep, but the French language is full of pitfalls for the inexperienced and he was further enraged when the voice said that it wasn't the butler, it was the conductor, and m'sieu's passport——

Logan switched out the light, threw himself back in the bed and covered his head with the bedclothes, but the quiet persistent tapping went on. He sprang up in a rage, switched on the light, flung open the door and was beginning: "I shall make a serious complaint——" when it dawned upon him that he was not looking at the homely features of the *chef de train* but the cold eyes and grim mouth of Yudin with the rat-face of Brachko peering round his shoulder. Logan recognized them at once and opened his mouth to yell for help, but Yudin gripped his throat and choked him into silence while Brachko held down the flailing arms. Logan left off struggling; Yudin let the limp body slip to the floor and Brachko shut the door and locked it.

"That's good," he said contentedly. "Now if we go through his things quickly we can be out again before he recovers."

"Recovers?" said Yudin.

6   *MONSIEUR LOGAN*

Yudin began by turning out the contents of one of Logan's suitcases upon the lower bunk, feeling all round the lining and even slitting it carefully in one or two places. "I don't think this lining has been disturbed," he said; "it takes an expert workman to put it in as neatly as this, I am just making sure. We will examine everything and pack it again. Wake up!" he added sharply. "What are you pawing him about for? He won't interfere."

"I was trying to feel his heart," said Brachko.

"You won't unless you cut him open. He's dead, you fool. Come and help me look through these things."

Brachko stood up and began to unfold Logan's things, examine them carefully and fold them up again. "Why are we taking all this trouble? I understood it was a large packet."

"It was, but he may have opened it and hidden each sheet separately." Yudin glanced at his watch. "Well, that one's done and they are not there. I suppose he hasn't got them on him, strapped to his body with sticking plaster? Lend a hand, Brachko. What's the matter? Moonstruck?"

"Are you sure he is really dead?"

"Of course he's dead. Look at him. Feel his pulse if you know how. Do you want Chadai here to give a death certificate? The man hasn't breathed for more than ten minutes." Yudin glanced at his watch again and·Brachko noticed it.

"Why do you keep on doing that?"

"Because in about five minutes or a little more this train will slow down to cross the marshalling yards at Hazebrouck. Trains don't run fast over numerous rail crossings and points, you know. Something might happen and railwaymen don't like that. It reflects upon their professional honour, you know. Besides, there's a row about it." Yudin was busily transferring odds and ends from the pockets of the long loose overcoat he wore into the pockets of the suit underneath; he then took off the overcoat. "It's a pity to sacrifice this coat but it's all in a good cause. I can buy another in Paris."

"What are you going to do?"

"Put this coat on him to cover his pyjamas, just in case someone looks into the corridor at the wrong moment. Then, when the train slows down, we walk him along the corridor between us, open the door and push him out."

"But," objected Brachko, "suppose somebody comes along the corridor just then?"

"Then we are all looking out of the window. He will be held up between us and we shall flatten ourselves to let whoever it is go by. But it's not likely."

"And why wait till the train slows down?"

"Help me lift him, he's heavy. I want his arm through this sleeve. We wait, my good Brachko, because it is quite easy to fall out of an open door on a swiftly moving train, especially if you are trying to push someone else out, and I have no ambition—hurry up, she's slowing down—to accompany him on to the metals. You can do as you like. Now the other arm."

"Are you really quite sure," said Brachko earnestly, "that he is dead?"

"Are you really quite idiotic?" asked Yudin. "For the fourth time, yes. Why?"

"He is still warm; he is quite limp too."

"Haven't you ever seen a corpse before?"

"Of course I have," said Brachko indignantly, "hundreds of them; that's why I ask. Haven't you? Corpses are quite cold, cold as stones and stiff; if you lift them they come up all in one piece. Not like this," he said, shaking Logan's arm; "look at his hand. It waggles."

"Now lift him up. Hold him under the arm and lift, that's right. Higher yet, you're letting him droop your side."

"He is too tall for me," complained Brachko.

"Well, do your best; we must go now or we shall be right in the station. Open the door."

Since Logan's compartment was at the end of the coach it was only a couple of yards to the outer door at the end. The conductor was not on his little seat at the end of the corridor—he does not sit there all night—no one came along or even looked out from any compartment. Yudin opened the outer door; there was an awkward shuffle for a moment and then Logan's body pitched forward down the steps and disappeared. Yudin shut the door again just in time as a goods engine, drawing a long string of clanking trucks, hissed past within a yard of them.

"There," said Yudin, pushing Brachko before him, "now are you satisfied he's dead?"

The Paris train, which had slowed to almost walking pace, now began to pick up speed. The two Russians continued their search of Logan's possessions and found nothing to interest them, not even in the suit hanging in the wardrobe, though they examined it with scrupulous care. Nor was there anything hidden in the compartment, though they searched both bunks, all the cupboards and under the carpet. At last even Yudin stopped hunting.

"They are not here," he said, "those designs."

"So he need not have been killed."

"Of course he had to die, why can't you think? He had recognized us, hadn't he? Now we tidy up thoroughly. Fold up that suit. Wait a minute, put these things in the pockets. Keys, handkerchief and so on off that little shelf. They were in those pockets, weren't they? You took them out. Sponge off the washstand——"

"What's the idea?" asked Brachko.

"To give the impression that he finished the journey, of course. They can hunt for him in Paris."

"They will find the body on the line."

"I never met your equal," said Yudin energetically, "for

making difficulties and suggesting obstacles. Of course they'll find the body on the line, but even if it's recognizable, which would surprise me, they won't connect it with a passenger who has apparently disappeared on arrival. At least, not till long after we're back in London. Put both cases on the bottom bunk, that's right. Now let's go and have a couple of hours' sleep, we've earned it."

"What shall we do when we get to Paris?"

"Go and report, of course. Probably they'll send us straight back to London, or we may be here a few days."

"I wouldn't mind if we did," said Brachko. "I don't care so much for London."

At twenty minutes past nine Laurence Logan strode into the Nord station in Paris just in time to see the foremost passengers coming along the platform from the Dunkirk ferry train. He paused, murmured that he supposed he'd better go right along to the train or Edward would be getting fussed, and went to buy himself a platform ticket. He turned away from the platform entrance just as the first passengers came streaming out, among them two Russians who seemed to be in haste. They almost ran out of the station, leapt into a taxi and were whirled away.

Laurence Logan returned to the barrier and had to push his way through the crowd outside it waiting to greet arriving friends; once through the barrier he had to struggle against the passengers themselves. He looked over people's heads, for he was as tall as his brother, but could not see anything of that other tall figure with the face so like his own. He walked along beside the sleeping-car coaches, looking up at the windows as he passed. He was already a little uneasy, since Edward was not a man to conjure up imaginary dangers, he had far too little imagination. Laurence, in spite of his casual manner on the telephone, had been unpleasantly impressed by Edward's words. Why wasn't Edward hopping on the steps of his coach impatiently awaiting him as usual?

He reached the last of the sleeping cars and turned back; at the doorway of the next one he was stopped by a man calling his name.

"M'sieu Logan! M'sieu Logan!"

He turned and ran up the steps into the coach, where the conductor seized upon him. "M'sieu, I have been seeking you in vain, there is your Customs declaration form not completed, I have here your passport, the Customs officers are waiting, did you not know it is strictly forbidden to leave the train until you have passed the Customs, I have been looking for m'sieu this half hour——"

Evidently there was something very wrong here; where was Edward? In the meantime the conductor had obviously taken him for the missing man; there was nothing new in that, they had been mistaken for each other all their lives. Laurence, who was extremely fluent in French, remembered that his brother was not. All the better; if he could pretend not to understand it would give him more time to think.

"I am sorry," he began in slow, awkward French. "I only got out to buy a paper." He indicated the *Daily Telegraph* under his arm which it was his habit to buy every morning. "I was coming back——"

He was hustled into his brother's compartment, all neat and tidy except for the rumpled bedclothes on the upper bunk. Two suitcases on the lower bunk were packed, but had their lids thrown back ready for the Customs examination; Laurence noticed them. "I am sorry," he repeated. "I left the cases open like that for the officers; I thought that would"—he hesitated for a French equivalent for "do" and selected "*faire*"—"*Je crois que ça sera faire*—and if that doesn't convince them," he added to himself, "nothing will."

"But m'sieu is English," said the Customs men, a phrase which excuses any idiocy and produces immediate assistance.

"Yes," said Laurence apologetically and maintained that character by heavily overtipping the conductor, who thanked him in the warmest terms. The three Frenchmen then went into committee to help him fill up his Customs declaration, leaving Laurence nothing to do but sign E. J. Logan along the bottom. He then handed out cigarettes all round and when one of the Customs men remarked that they were French, Laurence said that of course they were, he liked them, and they were in fact one of his motives for leaping out of the train as soon as it stopped.

"M'sieu has been in France before," said the other Customs officer kindly. Laurence said he had, on several occasions, but the last was some years ago. "I am horrified," he added, "to find my French so rusty——"

"It will come back," said the conductor, patting him on the arm, "m'sieu will find that it will all come back when he hears it spoken all around him."

"Do you not wish to go through my luggage?"

The Customs men said that nothing was further from their thoughts and took their leave with great friendliness while the conductor called up a porter. Laurence, left alone for a moment, looked rapidly and efficiently round the compartment. If something unpleasant had happened to Edward there might be bloodstains or some other sign of struggle. He was examining the bedclothes when the conductor came back.

"M'sieu has lost something?"

"No, no. I was only making sure I had not left a handkerchief under the pillow."

"Already m'sieu's French returns," said the conductor approvingly. "He hardly hesitated that time."

"I shall be quite fluent tomorrow," laughed monsieur, and closed the suitcases for the porter to take. Laurence did not, as a rule, wear a hat even in Paris; he picked up Edward's bowler, gloves and umbrella and asked the porter what the taxi situation was like in Paris these days, was there any chance of getting one?

He was driven to the St. Pétersbourg Hotel in the Rue Caumartin, conducted to the office and given a white form to fill up. This was simple, though Laurence hesitated for a moment over: "Reason for the journey: Business—Health—Pleasure (cross out whichever is inapplicable)" and decided upon Business, though Health was, he felt, more strictly accurate. It was natural to copy the particulars required out of Edward's passport, for who remembers the date and number of his own? He signed it Edw. J. Logan, having refreshed his memory of Edward's formal signature in the passport, and handed the white paper to those whose duty it was to copy the particulars (a) on a green form to be sent to the police within twenty-four hours and (b) into the hotel register. It is not known what becomes of the original white paper completed and signed by the traveller.

Logan was then taken upstairs to his room, number twelve on the mezzanine floor; it had the advantage of being at the top of one flight only, so that there was no need at any time to await an absent lift. Number twelve was a pleasant room, though its window looked out into a light well instead of upon the street; just below the window was the skylight of the dining room below, and round the edge of this a narrow path for the use of men cleaning the skylight. Laurence looked thoughtfully at it; it offered a possible escape route in case of emergency and he had no idea at all in what sort of an emergency Edward had become entangled. Selling peppers and spices appeared such a harmless and peaceful trade unless, as a result of the pepper shortage, someone had produced a recipe for synthetic pepper which was worth a fortune to its possessor and Edward had got it. There was a gang of ruffians, mused Laurence, waiting for the luggage to come up; ruffians subsidized by rival pepper firms in the City who were prepared to stop at nothing to wrest the Sneezo formula from poor Edward. Or perhaps Edward had stolen the formula and was fleeing before its justly indignant owner. Or possibly——

There was a tap at the door and Laurence abandoned his thriller plots to receive the luggage. He looked it over; there were the same two cases Edward always used, one slightly larger than the other but otherwise similar, with his name stamped upon the lids. Laurence opened the cases, thinking as he did so of how often he had met Edward upon arrival and come up to some hotel bedroom with him to wait while he tidied himself up after the journey before they went out to have dinner together. Edward used to turn the lids back carefully in order not to damage the hinges, and there on the top of the smaller case would be his sponge bag, shaving kit and hairbrushes, with his pyjamas next below that, all ready for——

They were not there. That is, they were not on the top, ready to be taken out and used first. Laurence stood back and looked at the case. Well, perhaps the faithful Greene had not packed them this time, perhaps he was away or ill and some hireling had taken his place. These things were not on the top of the larger case, either.

Laurence unpacked the smaller case first. Shirts, ties, collars, change of underwear all present and correct. He ran his finger along the side of the lining of the case and almost at once it caught upon something; he bent over and looked closely. The lining had been very carefully slit here and there, no more than was absolutely necessary to ensure that there was nothing hidden behind it. Judging by the space between the slits, the object sought was not so very small, say about the size of a half sheet of note paper.

He turned to the larger case which contained suits; it appeared to be rather tightly packed. A light raincoat on the top, a lounge suit, a dinner-jacket outfit complete, a second lounge suit. As he took this out something rattled in one of the pockets, some small change in English money. Laurence snatched up the coat and felt through all the pockets, laying the contents on the dressing table. Wallet containing five pounds in one-pound notes, two keys on a ring—the keys of the suitcases—a silver pencil, a packet of twenty Churchman's No. 1 with two cigarettes missing, a silver lighter with Edward's initials on it and a used handkerchief.

Laurence dropped the coat on the floor, sat down on a chair and lit a cigarette. It was one of Edward's most fixed habits—he had many—always to take everything out of his pockets when he took off his suit; even when they were little boys together Edward had done this in spite of being laughed at for a sissy. He was just as naturally methodical and tidy as Laurence was the reverse, and he had kept it up. Only the last time they were together when Edward was changing he had done this and Laurence had commented. "Why spoil the shape of your pockets?" said Edward reasonably. "It doesn't take a moment to empty them."

So this was the suit he had been wearing. Laurence sprang up suddenly and hunted through the piles of clothes on the bed. Pyjamas, where were they? There were none. So wherever Edward was and whatever he was doing, he was dressed simply in a pair of pyjamas, probably with brown stripes. Edward liked brown stripes. The dressing gown was there, also bedroom slippers and two pairs of shoes. In pyjamas and with bare feet . . .

There was something loose in the bottom of the second case and Laurence took it out, a silver engine-turned cigarette case without initials but with an inscription on the inside in facsimile of a neat feminine handwriting: "From Betty." The case contained half a dozen Russian cigarettes.

"Who the devil," said Logan aloud, "is Betty? A girl friend, I suppose, but why Russian cigarettes? Edward hated them. Or does this case belong to the fellow who searched the cases? He might have dropped it in when he was repacking— is this lining cut too? Yes."

Another thought occurred to him and he examined the suits. In each case the lining had been slit to uncover the padding in the shoulders.

Laurence abandoned his examination to go and stare unseeingly out of the window. Something had happened, and it had happened on that train. Not even in Paris does one walk out of a main-line terminus at half-past nine in the morning in pyjamas and with bare feet, not without attracting attention. Least of all a man like Edward, who was acutely unhappy if he were wearing the wrong sort of tie.

Would it be any good questioning the conductor of Edward's coach? Of course not; the man had accepted Laurence without hesitation as the Mr. Logan who had travelled that night. Nor had he appeared in the least surprised or embarrassed, as he certainly would have been if he had had a hand in whatever had been done.

As for the man's readiness to mistake him for his brother, there was nothing remarkable in that. They had always been ludicrously alike and still were, except for the odd marks and scars that a man acquires as time goes on and the difference in manner and bearing born of their very different modes of life. No casual acquaintance had ever known them apart.

Poor old Edward, honest, conscientious, kindly, a slave to habit and the world's most crashing bore. They had next to nothing in common, but the deep unreasoning tie of blood remained, even that closer tie which unites twins. Laurence's jaw came forward. Go to the police? No. He would see this through himself.

7

FEET IN THE FENDER

THOMAS ELPHINSTONE HAMBLEDON looked up from his desk as the door opened and Superintendent Bagshott came in.

"Hullo, Bagshott. Come in and sit down. What can we do for you today? A nice line in broken bottles from Glasgow or a fresh issue of subversive activities at Plymouth?"

Bagshott sat down, helped himself to one of Hambledon's cigars and said it was about that fellow Muntz.

"Muntz. Oh yes, the Herr Doctor of Physics Ignatius Muntz, originally of Heidelberg, and his ultra-sonic beam."

"Ultra——"

"Sonic. Beyond the range of audible sound, though the vibrations are such as would produce a sound if there were anyone capable of hearing it, if you see what I mean."

"Don't I remember hearing something about this in Germany,' 'said Bagshott, "towards the end of the war? One of Hitler's secret weapons? I thought it was all just yap."

"Oh no, it wasn't," said Tommy. "I mean, it was quite true that they were trying to produce a beam which, when turned upon people—or, more likely, when they walked into it— would disintegrate them or send them gaga. They got so far as producing the desired—er—influence, but they couldn't control it. Instead of getting a beam localized like a searchlight, the contraption radiated in all directions like a burning haystack, so that all the scientists concerned went gaga and it was understandably difficult to finish the job. I understand that dogs, when they meet an ultra-sonic—er—emanation, leap into the air and rush yelping away; presumably it is hoped that an opposing army will do the same. A scene of wild enchantment, don't you agree?"

"And Muntz is supposed to have found a means of controlling it?"

"That's the idea, though whether he really did is quite another thing. Why, has he turned up at last?"

"No. You remember you traced him as far as a ship from Rotterdam bound for Spain. He was taken off her in the Channel by some people in a cabin cruiser. We've traced the cabin cruiser."

"Receive my full-throated roar of approval and tell me all about it."

"The cabin cruiser," said Bagshott, lighting the cigar, "belonged to a man named Stephen Alton, ex-Navy hostilities-only; he kept her at Wapping. The river, dock and riverside police have had their eye on him for some time in connection with robberies from the dock area but they couldn't pin anything on him. Two days ago they got a line on him for a whisky robbery from a bonded warehouse, so when he was seen entering a block of offices behind City Road a couple of policemen went in to pick him up. They met him on the stairs and were bringing him down when three men who were standing in the entrance hall opened fire on them."

"I saw that in the paper," said Hambledon. "Three policemen, weren't there?"

Bagshott nodded. "The third was the police driver. One of them is still pretty bad but he won't die; the other two will be all right in a matter of days. Alton escaped in the police car and the three men in the hall ran out and disappeared for the time. Now Alton's body has been picked out of the river by the River Police, who recognized it. He had been tortured, Hambledon."

"Died under it?"

"According to the p.m., he died of heart failure; his injuries were not severe enough in themselves to kill him. Well, the Wapping police went to pick up his crew, but they have all scattered except the second engineer, who was living peaceably at home with his mother. He is a new hand and it seems quite likely that he didn't know what Alton was actually doing. He identified Alton without hesitation and was quite willing to talk, especially when he had been shown the —er—evidence. Asked if he knew any possible reason, however vague, why anyone should torture Alton, he told a long and detailed story about taking a chap off a ship in mid-Channel one stormy night. The dates and description match, I've no doubt myself that it was Muntz, but I daresay you'll want to interview this man yourself. Muntz—let's call him that—was carrying a brief case containing papers which he said were worth vast sums to the Russians and when the British Government saw them they would dance ring-o'-roses round Nelson's Column. So said the second engineer."

"Muntz, all right," said Hambledon.

"Very well, then. This fellow says it was one of the roughest nights he was ever out in and the boat was doing everything but turn somersaults. Muntz was overcome by seasickness and went up on deck to get the fresh air and hang over the rail. A little later, when this young chap went up to look for him, he'd disappeared. Fallen overboard, apparently; it seems that it would have been more than possible."

"What became of the brief case and the papers?"

"The second engineer said he wondered that, but Alton was not a man one questioned about what wasn't one's business. He said it was his first trip and the papers were the skipper's responsibility anyway——"

"He's right there, of course. I'll see him sometime," said Hambledon, "when you've done with him."

"There's something else," said Bagshott. "When Alton drove off after the police were shot, the three men who did it also ran out, as I said. We have now found somebody who saw them jump into a grey saloon car, parked round the corner, and drive away. Our informant, a woman, didn't know the make or number of the car but she did know the driver, one Mick Cutler. We know Mr. Cutler; we think he is, or was, the driver for a gang of car thieves. What is more, for a short time before that he had been driving a grey saloon car for private hire. Later in the evening of the day the shooting took place—two days ago; that was Tuesday, then—a grey saloon car was found abandoned on a bombed site in Pimlico, having had the number plates removed and the engine number filed off."

"And where is Cutler?"

"We're looking for him and I imagine we shall find him. He was in Bermondsey early this morning. He lives there."

It was quite true that Mick Cutler lived in Bermondsey; he rented a room in a house belonging to a widow. He was also courting the widow; she was older than he but she owned a house; besides, if one is courting the householder one is not confined to one's bed-sitting-room. One sits in the kitchen with one's feet in the fender, which is so much pleasanter.

He also had a place of business tucked away in the bombed area near Jamaica Road. It consisted of one large corrugated-iron shed on a levelled space behind a row of uninhabitable houses; the way in to the shed was down an alley between two of the houses, an alley so narrow that one would not think a car could pass along it. At the end there was a sharp left-hand turn so acute that even Cutler could not get a car round without backing; after that there came a right-hand turn into the shed doors and here the space was so constricted that the only way to get a car in was to jack up the back wheels and then push it sideways till the jack fell over and the back wheels had been moved a foot or so to the left. In short, it was so nearly impossible to get a car in there at all that the police never bothered to look, which was as well for Cutler, since it was here that stolen cars were resprayed a different colour and fitted with different number plates. There was an air compressor complete with paint sprayer in one corner of the shed, another corner at the far end was partitioned off into a small office with a fixed desk, a chair and a couple of shelves holding some dusty files, a pile of road maps and one each of the A.A. and R.A.C. handbooks.

Cutler spent the morning clearing up after the last job, cleaning out the paint sprayer and tidying up generally. There was no car in at that moment but Cutler had good reason to think that if all went well there would be one tomorrow night. He had told the widow he would be home to dinner at midday; he washed his hands in a pail of paraffin and went out, locking both the office door and the postern in the big outer doors.

He walked home, since it was no great distance, and was just about to turn the last corner into the street where he lived when a small and dirty boy dashed up to him.

"Look out—cops!"

"What?"

"Cops arstin' for you—comin' this way—come in 'ere."

They rushed in at the open door of the house they were passing at the moment and the door was shut and locked. A cautious voice called down the stairs:

"That you, Ernie?"

"Yes, mum, an' I got 'im!"

"Good boy." The woman came down the stairs. "Mrs. Lake's Annie come round sayin' the cops was at your 'ouse arstin' for you, so I guess you'd best stop 'ere for a bit."

He stayed there till well after dark, since the police continued to obstruct the passage of free men by hanging about all day and inconveniently looking round corners. Bulletins from the front were brought in at intervals by the children of the district, artfully careful not to be seen entering the house. Between ten and eleven at night Cutler watched his opportunity and slipped away, leaving a message for the widow that he would sleep elsewhere till things settled down. He went back by devious routes to his workshop; there were some sacks there, he could sleep on the office floor for tonight and go further away tomorrow.

The workshop was all in darkness as expected. He locked the postern door after himself and, by the light of matches, closed the lightproof shutters which he had fitted over the windows. He made his way to the office door, unlocked it and switched on the light——

Chadai was sitting on the chair inside, Chadai as unruffled, composed and well-groomed as ever with his gold-rimmed spectacles upon his face.

Cutler gasped for breath, clutched the doorpost and gasped again.

"You seem surprised," said Chadai calmly. "I have been waiting here for you for"—he glanced at his watch—"nearly three hours."

"Sittin' there in the dark—with your spectacles on——"

"Why not? Do you know the police are after you?"

"Course I do. I been 'iding from 'em all day."

"I have come," said Chadai, "to help you in your predicament. There is a ship coming into the docks tonight; I will tell you where to find her, the *Kalisz*. You will make your way to her tomorrow; you need not fear a search, they will hide you. You will be better out of this country for a time, you agree with me, I am sure."

"Th-thank you for the kind thought——"

"Here is some money." Chadai stood up, took a thick wad of notes out of an inner pocket and gave them to Cutler. "You see, if you stay here the police will catch you and then you will talk. I cannot have talk, that is why I am giving you money."

Cutler was examining the notes. "What are these, they ain't English."

"They are Polish."

"Besides, I don't want money, thanks a lot all the same. I've got some, see? That's what I come 'ere for, mainly."

Cutler crouched down and levered up one of the floorboards with his knife. Underneath was a tin box almost full of pound and ten-shilling notes held together by rubber bands. "Plenty of money," he said, straightening up with the notes in his hand. "As I say, thanks a lot, but—"

"Those will be of no use to you in Poland," said Chadai patiently.

"I'm not going to Poland. What's the use of me going there; I can't speak their lingo, I don't know their ways and if I put a foot wrong it'll be me for a concentration camp to be starved and worked to death. No, mister, I ain't going."

Chadai sighed, picked up the Polish money and put it in his pocket. "You will not go abroad, you will stay here, then, your mind is made up?"

"That's right, mister. As I say—"

"Stay here, then!" snapped Chadai, and shot him through the head. The Russian looked round to make sure he had left no traces of his presence, stepped over Cutler's body and switched out the light. He had a small electric torch which guided him to the postern door; he unlocked it, locked it again after him, and walked quietly away in the darkness.

Three days after Edward Logan's flight to Paris the police station at West Kensington received a telephone call from a lady who complained that her flat had been broken into during her absence at business and would somebody please do something. The desk sergeant reassured her and the Inspector detailed a young detective sergeant to go round and see what had happened. "Name of Allen," he said, and added the address. "First-floor flat."

When the detective sergeant arrived at the front door and looked at the cards over the different bells he found that the first-floor tenant's name was Alton, not Allen. He paused for a moment, remembering a general order that any stray gleam of light which might fall upon one Stephen Alton, recently deceased, was to be reported at once direct to Superintendent Bagshott at Scotland Yard. This was a Miss Elizabeth Alton, not a common surname. He rang the bell, and Betty Alton, who had been watching him from the window, ran downstairs to let him in.

"Miss Alton? I am Detective Sergeant Waller of the Metropolitan Police. I understand you have had some sort of trouble here?"

"Please come up," said Betty Alton. "I am so glad to see you; this sort of thing is rather frightening when one lives alone. This is my flat, see for yourself."

There was certainly plenty to see, for the flat had been thoroughly and systematically ransacked. When the Russians had searched it at the time they took Stephen Alton, they had merely turned out cupboards and drawers, assuming that Alton had brought the packet with him a quarter of an hour earlier and that therefore it would be only superficially concealed. Betty had tidied up after them, swept up broken glass and china and sewn up slits in the chair covers. This time the search had been much more thorough and damaging. In addition to throwing on the floor everything which cupboards and drawers contained, heavy furniture had been pulled away from the walls, the pictures had been taken down and ejected from their frames and every piece of padding in the flat from Betty's mattress to the stuffed seats on her two dining-table chairs had been slashed open and the insides dragged out. The carpets had been pulled up and thrown in a heap over the table.

"Oh dear, oh dear," said Waller sympathetically, "this is a horrid sight, it is really."

The sympathy was a mistake, for Betty sat down heavily on the nearest chair and burst into tears. Waller left her to it and walked round the flat looking at the devastation; he paused in the kitchen long enough to put the kettle on and came back.

"Could you tell me, madam, whether there is anything missing?" The deliberately official tone had its effect; Betty wiped her eyes and sat up. "If you have any jewellery or other valuables—money——"

"In my bedroom, a few things—I'll go and see."

"I hope you'll forgive me, madam, when I was in the kitchen I took the liberty of putting the kettle on. I thought a nice cup of tea——"

"You are very kind," said Betty.

"You live here alone, you said? Have you any relations anywhere handy?"

"My brother is the only relation I have and he's away at the moment."

"That's a pity. Can you get in touch with him?"

"I—I don't think so, I don't know his address at the moment. You see, he travels a lot and he's just gone away again. I shall hear from him—oh, any time now."

"Well, now, if I might have a few particulars," said Waller, and brought out his notebook. "The usual tiresome formalities, you know."

The usual tiresome formalities include her brother's name and the address of the boardinghouse near Liverpool Street where he lived when he was at home. When these were completed Waller asked if she had touched anything in the room since she came in.

"Oh, I don't know, why? Oh, fingerprints, I suppose. I used the telephone to ring you up."

"Naturally. Of course you did. Still, I don't think we'll use it again just yet. I saw a telephone box just at the corner; I'll go and ring up my superiors from there and perhaps while I'm doing so you'll just make sure if your valuables are safe, and then perhaps that kettle will be boiling, what? I won't be more than a few minutes."

"You are very kind," she said again, and he went out of the flat to report to Bagshott. "Her brother's name is Stephen, the address is the same and she doesn't know where he is at the moment but she evidently has no idea he is dead—if it is the same man," said Waller.

"I'll bring the fingerprint experts along with me and examine the place thoroughly," said Bagshott. "Don't say anything more to the woman; I am coming along myself at once." He put down the receiver and immediately lifted it again to ring up Hambledon. "The late Stephen Alton apparently had a sister whose flat has been ransacked this afternoon."

"Oh, really," said Hambledon. "Looks rather as though he didn't talk in spite of the treatment, doesn't it? Are you going there, wherever it is? West Kensington. Call for me on your way, won't you?"

"Stephen Alton is her brother," said Bagshott when Hambledon got into the car. "The address she gave as his is the place where he lived—I mean where the dead man lived."

"When he was alive, yes."

"And she doesn't know he's dead."

"Oh," said Hambledon. "In that case, if you'll drop me at a tobacconist's near the flat I'll walk on and join you in a few minutes. I want some cigarettes."

"Don't worry, I've got plenty," said Bagshott and added: "Coward," as an afterthought.

"I don't like weeps," explained Hambledon.

"Think of all the weeping you've occasioned and haven't seen," said Bagshott callously, "that'll level things up."

8   *THE MARBLE GENTLEMAN*

WHEN THEY went upstairs to the flat they found Waller standing about near the door and Betty Alton, red-eyed but calm, drinking tea. The finger-print expert and his attendant photographer got to work at once and Bagshott introduced himself.

"I am Superintendent Bagshott and this is Mr. Hambledon. Miss Alton, is there anywhere where we could have a quiet talk for a few minutes?"

"There's the kitchen," she said; "it's very small but it isn't such a mess as this room. There's only one chair in it but there's another in the bathroom and——"

"We'll manage," said Bagshott, shepherding her along, "we'll manage. I'm sure the kitchen will do perfectly. Do you smoke?" he added as they settled round the kitchen table with Hambledon perched on the bathroom stool. "Let me offer you a cigarette, that's right. I've got a lighter. There. Now, Miss Alton, I am very sorry to have to say that I'm afraid we've got some bad news for you. I'm quite sure that you will be brave and help us in every——"

"Stephen?" she whispered.

"He had a cabin cruiser at Wapping——"

"For pity's sake tell me."

"He is dead, Miss Alton. His body was taken out of the river early this morning."

"Then those horrible men killed him. Oh, I knew they would, I warned him, I begged him to go to the police but—— Oh, this is too much! To have my flat wrecked twice inside a week and now you tell me they've killed poor Steve, oh, Steve—Mother, I did my best—Steve——"

Hambledon looked reproachfully at Bagshott and edged his stool as far as possible into the corner. Bagshott waited until the storm of sobbing had slowed down and then spoke in an authoritative voice.

"Miss Alton. I can't tell you how sorry I am to be the bearer of such bad news. But it is quite evident that you know a great deal which would help us in finding the criminals. If you could manage to answer a few questions I should be so very grateful."

Betty Alton looked at him for a moment. "Very well. I'll tell you all I know. There's no point in keeping secrets any longer. Can I have a drink?"

"Anything you like——"

"Just water, thanks, I'm thirsty. Where do you want me to start? When the Russians came in?"

"What Russians?"

"The ones who shot the policemen the other day."

"Is that really the beginning of the story?" asked Bagshott.

Betty Alton took a long drink of water from the glass Hambledon had filled for her, took a clean handkerchief from a pile of ironing on the dresser to dry her eyes, and began.

"I think it all started when he got hold of some drawings belonging to the Russians, somebody had brought them out of Russia. I don't know how Steve got hold of them——"

She had had a sound secretarial training and could give a clear account of events in their order. Bagshott took notes and did not interrupt more than was absolutely necessary; at the mention of "half a million" he raised his eyebrows but made no comment. She went unhesitatingly through everything that Stephen had told her that evening before the Russians entered the flat; it was only when she went on to describe their search of the flat for "a packet, not so small" that the account faltered and Bagshott's long years of experience told him that she was suppressing something.

"You are sure they didn't find anything?"

"Quite sure. That's why they took Steve away. They said they would make him tell them where it was. Besides, if they'd got it they wouldn't have come back today, would they?"

"No. Do you know where it is—the packet, I mean?"

"I haven't the faintest idea. Believe me, if I'd known I would have told them myself."

Bagshott nodded.

"Now, are you quite sure you've told us everything that happened?"

She nodded, but the policeman's sixth sense told him she was lying.

"And there were—how many people in the flat?"

He was on the right track, she didn't like that question. It wasn't a thing she was keeping quiet about, it was a person.

"There was my brother, and me, and the three Russians——"

"Nobody else?"

"Only a friend of mine who had called to see me," she said unwillingly, "but he had nothing whatever to do with it. Even the Russians saw that and they let him alone."

Bagshott tried to conjure up a picture of some man so patently innocent in every respect that even the Russians didn't suspect him, and failed completely.

"What is his name?"

"I don't want to tell you," she said desperately. "He is a City merchant of good standing and greatly respected. I don't want him dragged into this sordid case. Can't we leave him out of it? He has been endlessly kind to me and wants to marry me, but I wouldn't while Steve was—while I'd still got Steve. You never knew what Steve was going to do next; I was ashamed, I never even told him I'd got a brother. You know what Steve was," she ended lamely, "don't you?"

"I think you have had more than your share of trouble, Miss Alton, and believe me, I do sympathize. But don't you see——"

"I did my best to keep Steve straight, but nobody could," she said tearfully. "I promised Mother, but I suppose he was made like that."

"Some of them are," said Bagshott, "some of them are. Born with a kink. I am sure you did all you could."

"Oh, I did! Even when he was a little boy——"

"Yes, I'm sure of it. Reverting to the other gentleman, don't you see that if the Russians don't find what they want they may attack him?"

"They don't know who he is."

"But your brother might have told them after he left here, you know. Your brother knew who he was, of course?"

"He may have guessed——"

"But if they were both here at once, didn't you introduce them to each other?"

"No, I didn't. I didn't have an opportunity, actually. But I'm sure Steve wouldn't tell them, he wouldn't do a thing like that, ever. He wasn't honest, I know, but not like that. Why, when he was at school there was a boy who——"

"Let's get this straight, shall we?" said Bagshott. "When you say you had no chance to introduce them, do you mean the gentleman came in after the Russians were in the room?"

"I think he must have done," she said vaguely. "They were searching the place, one of them was holding Steve up with a gun, I was terrified and upset and suddenly I looked up and there he was, right in front of me. I—it was very silly, but it seemed the last straw after keeping quiet about Steve all this time and there he was right in the middle of the worst of it—I fainted."

"I see. And when you came round?"

"They had all gone. The Russians, I mean, and Steve. I think they'd only just gone; I seem to remember hearing them go, and the door shutting. Edw—the gentleman said it was all right, they'd gone."

"So you don't know what the Russians said to him, really, do you? If you were unconscious from the moment he came in until after they left?"

She stared at him. "Well, no. But I'm sure they didn't suspect him. No one would."

"He must have been a very impressive figure," said Hambledon, speaking for the first time.

"Oh, he is," she said simply. "Besides, you could see they hadn't touched him at all; he was still perfectly tidy as always, not a hair out of place, as they say." She giggled nervously.

"I'm sorry to be so persistent," said Bagshott, "but you must see that he is the only one who can tell us what happened during the time you were unconscious, and something might have been said which would unlock the whole thing if only we knew it. I cannot see what you are afraid of. He knows about your brother now; presumably you told him when you came round? Yes; well, as you say, he knows the worst of it and the most that can possibly happen so far as we are concerned is that he might possibly be called to give very brief evidence about what happened during that five or ten minutes; I don't suppose it was more from what you say. He must give evidence if required; it's his duty as a citizen, you know that. If he's done nothing to be ashamed of, it won't hurt him. If I were in your place I should be much more afraid of what those Russians will do if we can't catch them."

She sat in silence for a moment and then said: "Very well. Mr. Edward Logan. He is a spice importer with an office in Mincing Lane. His private address is Caroline Mansions near Regent's Park; you'll find both in the telephone directory."

"Thank you very much indeed," said Bagshott. "I'm sure you have acted wisely. He went away, did he, soon after the Russians went? Yes, I see. Have you seen him since?"

"No. No, I haven't. He was very kind that evening, but I'm afraid he—he may be disgusted. In any case, I've been busy. I've not been working for some time, owing to ill-health, but I have got a new post now, I started there today."

Bagshott asked for a description of the three Russians. The one who talked English—and very good English with only a slight foreign accent—was a man of about fifty with a smooth, rather plump face, smooth fair hair retiring from his temples and a short fair beard. He was about five feet seven inches in height, solid rather than stout in body and wearing gold-rimmed spectacles. "If he'd been English," said Betty, "I would have said he was a professional man rather than in business, a schoolmaster or a dentist or a bank manager, perhaps. Oh, he quoted Latin, or what I thought was Latin, and said something about a classical education."

Betty Alton was much less definite about the other two. The one who had held up Steve with a gun while the others searched the flat was a weaselly little rat of a man, dark-haired, with dark eyes too near to a long thin nose. Not very tall, no, definitely short. The third man was taller than either, nearly as tall as Mr. Logan, with a horrid face. Pressed to say what she meant by "horrid," Betty said he looked cruel. Not ugly, no, just dangerous. Colourless hair and pale eyes and a wide thin mouth. High cheekbones and his jawbones prominent.

Asked about their dress, Betty said that the spokesman was wearing a very nice lounge suit which fitted him exactly. An English suit, undoubtedly, and not a cheap one, either. The others' clothes were not so good and looked foreign. "Oh, by the way, they called the little one Peter. I don't really remember the other two very clearly, only the one who talked. He was the leader, I expect that's why."

Bagshott asked a few more questions to clear up minor points, told Betty that if—with a glance round the wrecked flat—she changed her address she must notify the police, and went away with Hambledon, leaving the fingerprint expert and the photographer to finish their monotonous task.

"Well, you got quite a lot out of that, didn't you?" said Hambledon. "Where do we go from here?"

"To Logan's flat," said Bagshott, giving the police driver the Caroline Mansions address.

"To see the marble gentleman."

"The marble gentleman?"

"Didn't you get that impression? One whom even the Russians could not suspect suggests to me the statue of Palmerston or Canning or whoever it is in a white marble frock coat on a pedestal in Parliament Square. With ponderus but stupendous dignity he descends from his rostrum nd his marble footsteps shake the ground like the statue of he Comandante in *Don Giovanni*, striking sparks from the avement and awe into the hearts of all beholders, even a rio of Russian thugs who don't even respect the police."

"I should be happier in my mind," said Bagshott, "if I were uite sure they did respect Logan. She doesn't know what appened after she fainted, if she did faint."

"But, you forget, he was quite unruffled afterwards in very way. Even his whiskers were not tousled."

"Whiskers?"

"Sorry, I'm still thinking of Canning, or is it Palmerston? he did say that he hadn't a hair out of place. Have we rrived?"

"This is Caroline Mansions, sir," said the police driver.

Hambledon got out, followed by Bagshott, who asked the ommissionaire which flat was Mr. Logan's.

"On the third floor, sir."

"Do you happen to know if he is at home?"

"I understand as Mr. Logan's abroad, sir, in Paris, I believe, ut 'is manservant will tell you. Here's the lift, sir, if you'll indly shut both doors and press the button marked third——"

Hambledon and Bagshott rose like Elijah out of sight, eached the third floor and knocked at Logan's door. No ne came to it and they knocked again.

"Must be out," said Bagshott.

"Listen," said Hambledon, who had remarkably quick hear-ng. Bagshott laid his ear against the panel.

"Sounds like a dog whining," he said, "only there's a bump-ng noise too."

Hambledon applied his ear also to the door panel. "Sounds ike a bee in a bottle to me. Also, such noises do men produce vhen they have been gagged."

The lift was still waiting behind them; Bagshott dived into t and took it down to ground level. The commissionaire came orward and Bagshott said: "Does Mr. Logan keep a dog?"

"No, sir. No dogs allowed 'ere, sir."

"Oh. Are you sure the manservant is in?"

"Well, fairly sure, sir. He went up, oh, 'bout four o'clock nd said as he was going to 'ave a nice quiet evening."

"You have passkeys to all these flats, have you? Well, bring hem along and we'll go up."

"I beg your pardon, sir, you are——"

Bagshott showed his card, the commissionaire sprang to

attention and the lift practically simultaneously, and they went up to the third floor again. Logan's door opened without difficulty and the commissionaire threw it wide.

"Good Lord alive and watchin', look at that!"

9 MUCH-PUBLICIZED NUMBER

THE PICTURE presented was very like that which they had looked upon earlier in Betty Logan's flat with one addition. There was a central-heating radiator against the opposite wall and a wooden chair was tethered to this. Upon the chair a figure was sitting; it was impossible to recognize it because it was covered by the hearthrug, which had been thrown right over it so that the only part visible was the lower eighteen inches or so of two naked human legs. These were kicking and winding round each other; from beneath the rug came also the whining noise which had been audible through the door. Bagshott and Hambledon carefully lifted the rug away and disclosed a man, naked as the day he was born, lashed to the chair and having his mouth closed up with adhesive tape.

They cut the cords and released him; he himself pulled the tape away from his mouth and only then did the commissionaire, standing thunderstruck in the doorway, recognize the man.

"Greene!" he cried. "Good lor', man, who done that?"

Greene snatched up his clothes which were lying in a heap on the floor and began in frantic haste to dress himself. Bagshott turned to the commissionaire.

"You know who I am, Superintendent Bagshott of Scotland Yard. Go downstairs now to your usual post in the hall and stay there till I call you up again. In the meantime you will not say one word to anyone of what you have seen here. Understand?"

"Yes, sir," said the commissionaire, saluting, "certainly, sir." He turned smartly about and marched out of the flat, shutting the door behind him.

Bagshott turned to Greene, who had, by then, at least covered his skin, and said: "Are you hurt?"